Tiny Temptations
FOUR HOLIDAY NOVELLAS

Tiny Temptations

Copyright © Ella Dominguez, 2018

All rights reserved

First Edition: February 2016
Revised Edition: February 2018

This book is a work of fiction. Any resemblances to actual persons, living or dead, events or places are entirely unintentional or coincidental. Names, characters, places and incidents are either the product of the author's imagination or are used fictitiously.

This ebook is licensed for your personal enjoyment only and may not be resold or given away to other people. If you would like to share this book with another person, please purchase an additional copy for each reader. If you are reading this book and did not purchase it, or it was not purchased for your use only, then, technically, you have stolen it and/or pirated it and are a despicable human being. Return to an ebook retailer and purchase your own copy.

No part of this book may be reproduced, scanned or distributed in any printed or electronic form without written consent of the copyright owner.

Thank you for respecting the hard work of this author.

ISBN-13: 978-1985698130
ISBN-10: 1985698137

ELLA DOMINGUEZ

TABLE OF CONTENTS

F#ck You Valentine!	6
F#ck You Valentine! Acknowledgements	7
F#ck You Valentine! Playlist	8
F#ck You Valentine! Long Story Short	9
F#ck You Valentine! Chapter One	10
F#ck You Valentine! Chapter Two	16
F#ck You Valentine! Chapter Three	22
F#ck You Valentine! Chapter Four	31
F#ck You Valentine! Chapter Five	38
F#ck You Valentine! Chapter Six	45
F#ck You Valentine! Chapter Seven	51
F#ck You Valentine! Chapter Eight	57
F#ck You Valentine! Chapter Nine	63
English Scones	68
F#ck You Valentine! Epilogue	70
A Cub for Christmas	71
A Cub for Christmas: Acknowledgements	72
A Cub for Christmas: Playlist	73

TINY TEMPTATIONS

A Cub for Christmas: Long Story Short	74
A Cub for Christmas: Chapter One	75
A Cub for Christmas: Chapter Two	80
A Cub for Christmas: Chapter Three	87
A Cub for Christmas: Chapter Four	94
A Cub for Christmas: Chapter Five	98
A Cub for Christmas: Chapter Six	104
A Cub for Christmas: Chapter Seven	112
A Cub for Christmas: Chapter Eight	118
A Cub for Christmas: Chapter Nine	125
The 12 Kinks of Christmas	131
The 12 Kinks of Christmas: Acknowledgements	132
The 12 Kinks of Christmas: Creative	133
The 12 Kinks of Christmas: Festive & Ornery	136
The 12 Kinks of Christmas: Mysterious & Generous	140
The 12 Kinks of Christmas: Imaginative & Thoughtful	145
The 12 Kinks of Christmas: Comical & Considerate	150
The 12 Kinks of Christmas: Benevolent & Mine	154
Hard Candy for Christmas	163

Hard Candy: Long Story Short	164
Hard Candy: Acknowledgements	165
Hard Candy: Chapter One	166
Hard Candy: Chapter Two	172
Hard Candy: Chapter Three	177
Hard Candy: Chapter Four	180
Hard Candy: Chapter Five	184
Hard Candy: Chapter Six	189
Hard Candy: Chapter Seven	194
Hard Candy: Chapter Eight	200
Hard Candy: Chapter Nine	205
Hard Candy: Chapter Ten	208
Hard Candy: Chapter Eleven	212
Hard Candy: Chapter Twelve	216
Hard Candy: Chapter Thirteen	225
Hard Candy: Chapter Fourteen	229
More from Ella D.	233

TINY TEMPTATIONS

F#CK YOU VALENTINE!

Copyright © Ella Dominguez, 2016

All rights reserved

First Edition: February 2016

ELLA DOMINGUEZ

F#CK YOU VALENTINE! ACKNOWLEDGEMENTS

Loving, humorous and supportive at all times—this goes out to my husband, daughter & mother.

Thank you to my amazing beta readers who, without fail, come through. On short notice, these wonderful gals helped to make this book better: Amy, Dorothy, Becki, April, Yvonne & Terri.

To my loyal & supportive fans & fellow indie authors who have encouraged me to keep writing, I can never say thank you enough. As long as you keep reading 'em, I'll keep writing 'em.

TINY TEMPTATIONS
F#CK YOU VALENTINE! PLAYLIST

Kiss Off by **Violent Femmes**
Break My Stride by **Matthew Wilder**
Here Comes the Rain Again by **Eurhythmics**
I Guess That's Why They Call it the Blues by **Elton John**
That's All by **Genesis**
Maneater by **Hall & Oates**
Girls on Film by **Duran Duran**
The Reflex by **Duran Duran**
New Moon on Monday by **Duran Duran**
Hungry Like the Wolf by **Duran Duran**
Send Me an Angel by **Real Life**
Don't Stand So Close to Me by **The Police**
Every Breath You Take by **The Police**:
True by **Spandau Ballet**
Hard to Say I'm Sorry by **Chicago**
Hold Me Now by **Thompson Twins**

ELLA DOMINGUEZ

F#CK YOU VALENTINE! LONG STORY SHORT

Screw the hearts & flowers.

A letter brings Andrew and Claire together, but circumstances threaten to tear them apart. Set in 1984, and long before email, sexting, and selfies, this unconventional romance proves that the technology we've grown dependent on to find *The One* is no match for destiny. But only if honesty and truthfulness prevails, and for Claire *and* Andrew, the truth can be a scary thing, no matter how irresistible their bond is.

TINY TEMPTATIONS
F#CK YOU VALENTINE! CHAPTER ONE

Roses are red. Violets are blue. I hope you rot in hell, and your tiny dick falls off, too. FUCK YOU VALENTINE! Sincerely, Claire. P.S. Screw the hearts & flowers, and screw you, too!

Two sentences that carried the sentiment of a thousand words and a pair of fire-engine red lip prints glared back at Andrew. On the typewritten letter, the words *Be My* in front of Valentine had been X'd out in deceptively lovely handwriting and replaced with the venomous expletive. Still four days away, this early Valentine's Day gift was sure to ruin the intended recipient's day. He felt a bit sorry for whoever that was, though not too sorry considering they had obviously broken Claire's heart, or, at a minimum, pissed her off enough to resort to a lame attempt at poetry.

He reached for the interdepartmental envelope and immediately found the mailroom error. It wasn't the first time André's mail had been mistakenly delivered to him. Although, nothing this entertaining had ever crossed his desk since his employment began there, or *scandalous* seeing as the only Claire in the company he knew of was the boss's daughter and considering André's recent engagement. He'd never actually met Claire, but the other lawyers had warned him that she was strictly hands-off as per Mr. Carlyle's orders.

He stared at the lip imprint on the letter again. He'd never seen such a creative and sexy way of getting across the time-honored yet dreaded message of *eat-shit-and-die.* Those lips were damned sexy, and he *almost* wished the letter had been for him so that he could frame it. Perhaps he should frame it anyway. Now *that* would be entertaining. André would shit his tailored pants. On the other hand, so would the boss.

He contemplated whether or not he should hand-deliver the note when he remembered André had left before noon that Friday for a romantic weekend getaway with his fiancée. Evidently, Claire wasn't thrilled with the cancellation of her Lover's Day plans. Then again, maybe there was more to it than just canceled plans: perhaps she'd found out about his engagement. Andrew had no idea and the letter sure as hell didn't allude to anything except a clear case of animosity.

He couldn't blame her. André was a real piece of work, and it was no surprise to Andrew the man had received such a hostile letter. Hell, he'd probably received dozens of them in his lifetime. A womanizing asshole who believed the rules didn't apply to him, he was known for his could-give-a-fuck-less-attitude and his inability to keep his dick in his pants. Surely Claire knew that. Andrew had only been with the firm for three months, and even he knew of that man's reputation.

With no distinct plan in mind except to replenish his caffeine level, he gathered the letter and his favorite over-sized coffee mug—the one his mother had given him after graduation and read *I ♥ My Job, I ♥ My Job, I ♥ My Job, (I Need the $$).* It spoke volumes to his situation.

After making a pit stop in the break room for a refill, he put his law school education to good use by asking a few well-worded yet indirect questions and located Claire's whereabouts: *transcription.* Surprised the Big Man's daughter would be working in the bowels of the building and not in one of the nicer offices with a view of downtown Dallas, he deposited his coffee back at his workstation and ventured to the basement.

When he arrived, it was just as awful as he'd imagined. Fluorescent bulbs crackling overhead, the smell of old, musty paper, and the hum of recorded voices and clack of typewriter keys echoing down a long hallway all filled him with a sense of dread. He slid his hand into his tweed jacket to touch the letter and nearly turned to leave.

The long corridor leading to the small room reminded him of a creepy scene from *The Shining*. He'd seen it during his freshman year in college at the drive-in theater, and when he glanced back at the elevator, he half expected to see red blood oozing down the doors like in the movie.

He didn't recall much else from the film as he hadn't gone there to see Nicholson wield an ax, but rather with the intention of trying to bang Janie Meyers from the Kappa Gamma house. He had only gotten as far as copping a feel, but making it to second base hadn't made the night a complete waste.

Standing in that lonely hallway with the Fuck-Off John letter in his pocket, Andrew found it eerily ironic that Janie had essentially ended things with him in the same manner. And right around Valentine's Day no less. Though, to be fair, he hadn't lied to her or cheated on her. His only mistake had been acting like a pussy-whipped asshole and falling too hard for a girl who clearly didn't understand the concept of selflessness.

ELLA DOMINGUEZ

What a shitty, worthless holiday. What the hell was the point of it? Real love, the truest kind, should be celebrated every day, not limited to one twenty-four hour period marked on the calendar. At least, that was his opinion. Not that his opinion meant anything considering he'd never actually been in love. Not *true* love, anyway.

Just as he resolved to leave without returning the letter, the sound of a woman's voice from behind startled him. So lost in his thoughts, he hadn't even heard her sneak up on him.

"Are you lost?"

When he spun around, the brightest green, almond-shaped eyes stared back at him. Adjusting his posture, he put on his best show of professionalism.

"No. I'm looking for Claire."

The sexy pout of her glossed, full lower lip intensified as her eyes narrowed. "Like, what do you want with *her*?"

Momentarily taken aback with her question and scent that was anything but the usual cheap perfume the rest of the female staff wore, his eyes roamed over her face and body. While dark, wispy bangs that touched her forehead gave her the appearance of innocence, the straight line of her jaw suggested stubbornness, as did the flash of mischievousness in her irises. A pastel pink cashmere sweater clung to her small breasts; gray pin-striped slacks encased her long, slender legs, and red patent-leather short pumps adorned her feet.

Her attire, catty tone and stance, with her hip cocked and one hand resting on it while giving him the evil-wary-eye, all reminded him of those holier-than-though types.

TINY TEMPTATIONS

When his gaze met hers, the slightest arch of her eyebrows let him know she had noticed his not-so-subtle attempt at checking her out.

He casually cleared his throat and adjusted his black, horn-rimmed glasses on his nose before answering. "*Like*, I have something that belongs to her," he mimicked her tone.

"Is that right?" Sarcasm littered her statement, and though she'd done a good job of hiding her Southern drawl with her previous statement, Andrew quickly picked up on it this time around.

Tired of her Little Miss Valley-Girl-Wannabe attitude, he thrust his hand into his pocket and retrieved the note. When he waved it front of her face her eyes widened, and the flush of her cheeks signaled annoyance.

The dark-haired woman who looked to be in her early twenties snatched the letter from his hand. "You opened her mail?"

Her accusation set him on edge and defensiveness laced his quick comeback. "It wasn't intentional. If Claire has a problem with it, tell her to take it up with the mailroom."

He spun back around and punched the elevator button before facing the woman again. "And tell her that she deserves a better man than André Heroux."

"You don't even know her," she hissed.

"I don't have to know her to figure out she deserves respect and truthfulness."

With his statement hanging in the air like a thick mist, he climbed onto the elevator and left the attractive yet aggravating woman standing in the hallway with her mouth hanging open. When the doors closed, he couldn't help but smile. *Stunned* was a good look on her. With any luck, and when she wasn't feeling so protective of her coworker, maybe he could get to know her a little better and *stun* her with more than just his verbal skills.

TINY TEMPTATIONS
F#CK YOU VALENTINE! CHAPTER TWO

The last of Andrew's coworkers had left him to finish the paperwork on his first major case by himself. He wasn't thrilled to be defending a man accused of grand larceny, especially when the evidence was so overwhelming, but he reminded himself that this experience would pave the way for his future dream career as an assistant district attorney. At any rate, he was damned lucky to have been hired by such a prestigious Texas law firm, regardless of their reputation for taking on some of the vilest criminals as clientele. All the experience he would gain as a defense attorney, he would later turn around and use to his advantage.

With his case files in hand, he gathered his coat and keys while trying to put out of his mind the fact that his Valentine's Day weekend would be spent alone, *again,* and that the rest of his colleagues had deserted him for a weekend of sexual frolicking. *Licking* being the operative part of that word. It was sad really, no, *pathetic,* that he would be building a defense for a man who had broken the law, rather than wining and dining some beauty. And not because of some overly-sentimental bogus holiday that encouraged the giving of cheap chocolates, overpriced flowers, and throw-away stuffed animals all in the name of getting a piece of ass—but because he meant it.

But then again, on his salary, Boone's Farm and Big Macs weren't exactly the food of the gods or something a woman would likely find romantic and/or appealing.

Security was waiting to lock up after him when he found the same woman whom he'd met in the Kubrickian hallway, standing just outside the front door and staring up at the moon. She hadn't seen him, and when a cool Texas breeze blew past them, she wrapped her arms around herself for warmth.

"Wearing a coat in winter is customary. Even in Texas," he commented at her lack of appropriate seasonal attire. She turned her body and her mouth popped open as if to deliver some quick jibe, but when she saw him, she said nothing. "Why are you out here, alone?"

"Not that it's any of your business, but I'm waiting for security to walk me to my car," she stated as her eyes darted up and down the length of his body.

"I'll wait with you until they come out."

"How chivalrous of you."

Though her response seemed courteous on the outset, her patronizing tone was ill-disguised. Andrew couldn't help but smirk. Her attempts at sounding and appearing unaffected were lame, but not as lame as her efforts at hiding her drawl. Though he couldn't figure out why anyone would want to hide that. Hell, they were living in the heart of Southern Drawl Country, what was the point? Besides, he found it charming. *To a degree*. It had taken some getting used to, but it was a nice change from the New York accent he'd grown up hearing. So was the mild climate.

Come to think of it, she hadn't mentioned his accent at all. That was usually the first thing Texans commented on when they spoke with him. Maybe he was losing it. He rolled his eyes at himself. That was doubtful. Born and raised in New York, his accent wasn't going anywhere unless he intentionally tried to lose it. And he wasn't about to.

When he readjusted his glasses on his nose, her eyes zoomed in on his face, and for the first time, the slightest hint of a smile touched her lips. It was a good look on her.

"You remind me of Christopher Reeve as Clark Kent."

Andrew bristled at her comment.

"A bumbling idiot?" he huffed, as he pressed the case files in his hand under his arm and averted his gaze to stare out at the street.

"I'm so sure," she stated with a roll of her eyes. "I mean in a sexy nerdy sort of way. You even have the same hair and eye color. You totally even dress the same way."

What he thought had been an insult turned out to be a compliment, and his defensiveness melted in a flash. Well, mostly a compliment considering Donner's version of Clark Kent had worn cheap suits, like him. Her pointing that out could be forgiven seeing as she had just said he was sexy, which was the closest thing to a woman flirting with him that he'd experienced since arriving in Dallas. When he glanced back at her, her half-smile remained.

"Like, hasn't anyone ever told you that?" she asked.

His eyes widened with exaggeration. "As if," he teased.

When she appeared to pick up on his mocking tone, a soft, disbelieving laugh slipped past her lips. She stared back at him as if unable to process that he wasn't impressed with her snobbish attitude, although he had no idea why. *Was anyone actually impressed with that?* He certainly wasn't. It didn't fit her and, frankly, her attitude seemed forced—like she was putting up a defensive wall around herself to scare people away.

With her wits apparently gathered, she finally responded and, thankfully, without an ounce of pretense.

"I'm surprised no one has told you that before."

"Not as surprised as I am that you're capable of acting friendly. After our little exchange this afternoon, I wasn't so sure that was possible. And as long as you continue to drop the whole Valley Girl BS, we might be able to have a real conversation."

Her cheeks brightened under the yellow hue of the front entrance lamp. "Sorry about that."

He liked this girl. The real one. The one with the bashful smile tipping her lips upward and genuine remorseful sentiment lacing her statement. The smile she was sharing with him, and the apology she'd given him, were the realest things he'd seen or heard from her.

"Did you give the letter back to Claire?"

Her eyes flicked from his mouth to his eyes and back. "Of course. It wasn't mine to keep."

"Mine either. That's why I returned it. I wonder if it's true about André's dick being tiny," he chuckled.

Her faint smile returned and widened, and she let out a burst of short laughter. "Just look at him. He looks like he has a tiny dick."

"That would explain why he screws around so much—he's trying to compensate for it."

Her smile vanished, and curiosity coated her question. "Why didn't you just give the note to him instead of returning it?"

TINY TEMPTATIONS

"I should have. I would have. I mean, I tried, but he left early. I didn't know what the hell else to do with it. Keeping it felt wrong."

Another gust of wind whipped past them, prompting him to set his files down on the ground just long enough to remove his coat and place it around her shoulders. When he did, her stunned look was back. It really was a great look on her. And he *really* liked being the one to have put it on her face.

"You know, Claire is damned lucky that letter ended up in my hands and not someone else's. Anyone else would have taken it straight to the boss," he continued when she stared up at him.

Just as she opened her mouth to say more, security came ambling out of the building. She gave him a resigned look that said she didn't want their conversation to end, and neither did he.

It occurred to him that he still didn't know who she was. "What's your name?"

Her thick, manicured brows pinched together, and she paused before glancing quickly at security as he approached her. "Give me a moment," she stated before she murmured in soft tones to the man. He nodded and walked away, leaving them alone on the curb. "Cece," she finally answered. "Walk me to my car?"

He agreed and followed behind her to the parking lot. When they arrived at her vehicle, he eyed it and whistled. "Nice wheels. How does someone on a typist's salary afford a new Dodge Daytona?"

"My folks got it for me," she whispered so softly he almost didn't hear her.

"They must really love you, Kiddo. My folks got me a used 1973 Pinto wagon—wood side paneling and all. Damn thing cost me nearly as much in repairs as my tuition fees."

She laughed, but her joy quickly turned into a frown as she handed him back his coat and pulled the keys from her pocket. "They didn't buy it out of love; they bought it as a bribe to get me to stay in law school."

He eyes widened and his jaw dropped. "You're in law school?"

Again, she shrugged her shoulders as she swung the car door open. "I didn't have much of a choice."

While she hovered in the door of her shiny red car, he threw caution to the wind. He knew dating someone he worked with, even if it wasn't someone in the same department, was a bad idea, but this girl did something to him. It was probably just a case of his libido doing the thinking, but he hoped it was more.

"It's early—how about we grab a bite to eat?"

Her mouth popped open, but she hesitated.

"Unless you have plans," he quickly interjected.

Her bright eyes sparkled under the three-quarter moon shining overhead. "I don't have any plans."

"Good, because I didn't feel like watching Hot Dog: The Movie alone for the third time."

The ornery lift of her brows when she said *I'll drive* and the smile that tipped the corners of her heart-shaped mouth upward were the sexiest damned things he'd seen in ages.

With any luck, the weekend wouldn't be spent alone after all.

TINY TEMPTATIONS
F#CK YOU VALENTINE! CHAPTER THREE

Seated in Cece's car, Andrew turned his head to watch her. She was attractive. More than that, she had a sort of exceptional beauty he didn't see often. Her wavy, medium-length dark, nearly black hair was offset by the most unique shade of jade-green eyes he'd ever come across. Tall and trim but not skinny, her height complimented his own, and her figure revealed she both took care of herself while not denying herself the pleasure of a good meal.

When she turned the ignition, the song *Kiss Off* blaring loudly through the speakers made him jump. Cece swiftly reached for her stereo and ejected the cassette while letting out a nervous laugh.

"Don't turn it off on account of me. I love the Violent Femmes," he commented as he pushed the tape back into the deck.

She glanced over at him and let out another discomfited chuckle as though she'd been caught doing something wrong. She kept her eyes on the road, her hands tightly gripped around the leather steering wheel, but while the song played, it was hard to miss the look of upset on her face.

"Is something bothering you?" he asked when the tune came to an end.

"It's nothing," she answered with a shake of her head, her upper-class Texas accent clearly audible. She promptly corrected herself. "It's. *Nothing*," she emphasized the last word while enunciating it more clearly and without the drawl.

Andrew couldn't resist asking, "Why do you do that?" When they came to a stop at a red light, she stared in confusion at him. "Try to hide your accent," he clarified.

"Because some people think it makes one sound uneducated," she answered flatly.

"Who the hell are these *people*? That couldn't be farther from the truth. Speaking imprudently about things one has no business speaking about is what makes someone sound uneducated, not their manner of speech, for fuck's sake. Whoever told you that needs to be told to fuck right off."

A broad grin reached from ear-to-ear, and she laughed. "I don't mean *all* accents, I mean a Southern accent."

"Oh, bullshit. Why in God's name would you want to sound like everyone else? Trying to hide who you are or where you come from is what's going to give people pause about you, not the inflection of your speech. Anyhow, I think your accent is charming. And damned sexy if you want to get down to brass tacks."

She let out another laugh. "Brass tacks? You sound like ..." She snapped her mouth closed, reached for the stereo and turned the radio on.

A few adjustments of the knob and *Break My Stride* filled the small space. Midway through the song, he pressed her to finish her question.

"I sound like *what*?"

"Like a lawyer," she answered with hesitancy.

Andrew got the impression her comment wasn't meant to be a compliment, but he decided to take it as one anyway. "Thanks. It's nice to know all those student loans for my education weren't a complete waste."

A short drive brought them to a diner not far from the firm, *Luke's B&B*. Andrew had visited it one other time, and as he recalled, they made one kick-ass fried pork burrito smothered in green sauce. That sort of food wasn't exactly conducive to keeping lean and fit, but he allowed himself the occasional splurge.

He scanned the restaurant for a booth and noted its interior resembled something out of the 1960's and was as lackluster as its patrons. Despite that, the smell of savory food drifting from the kitchen made his stomach rumble.

Leaning back into the cracked, red vinyl seat, he reached for a menu that was wedged between the napkin dispenser and a ketchup bottle. When the waitress arrived, Cece proved his theory right and ordered a hearty meal. He gave her a secret smile because nothing was more of a turn-off to him than some salad-eating-hoity-toity-fake-ladylike bullshit.

A glance out of the window revealed the first drops of rain dotting the pavement. As the rain picked up and small puddles began to form, the water reflected off the neon lights of the businesses that lined the street. The view outside, combined with the aromas of food and Cece's pricey perfume, brought on a sense of nostalgia for Andrew.

It had been a long time since he'd been on a date, or whatever this was. He missed it. School and studying had taken up so much of his time that his personal life had taken a back seat. Not to mention, he just flat out didn't feel like dealing with the same BS Janie had put him through. *Fuck all that*. He wouldn't even be thinking about her if it hadn't been for that damned letter and the made-up holiday that was right around the corner.

Thankfully, the waitress returned quickly with their drinks, pulling him out of his thoughts. With a glass pressed to her lips, Cece watched him closely as he removed his glasses to clean the lenses.

"Are you sure there's not a Superman costume beneath that shirt?"

His rugged facial features creased into a smile. If being compared to Mr. Reeve, aka The Man of Steel, was a sign of things to come, he'd hit some kind of jackpot. His heated gaze latched onto her and didn't go unnoticed on her part, and he savored the physical awareness that rippled between them. When he replaced the frames over his eyes, he saw an expression of playfulness fill her face as she set her beverage down.

"Some people say I remind them of Joan Jett."

"Why? Can you play the guitar and belt out a tune?"

"No," she laughed.

His stomach dropped. "Oh, shit. Are you a lesbian?"

Laughter barreled through her. "No! And Joan Jett is *not* a lesbian!"

He breathed a sigh of relief and laughed with her. "Like hell, she's not. You just wait, in twenty years it'll all come out."

She shook her head in disagreement. "I just mean people think I look like her."

"Nah. It's only because of your hair. You're way better looking than her."

Genuine elation shone in her eyes and her smile widened.

"How do you like law school?"

Her smile faded and her body stiffened. "I don't."

"Then why the hell are you doing it?"

Her frown deepened. "My folks insisted."

TINY TEMPTATIONS

"I can understand, but it's your life."

"That's what I said," she explained as her voice rose several octaves. "I told them I wanted to be a paleontologist, but they said digging up bones wouldn't pay the bills." Tears welled up in her eyes, but she blinked them back furiously and appeared agitated with her show of emotion. "They also said they wouldn't pay for college if I chose that major."

He could empathize with her frustration. His parents hadn't wanted him to go to law school—they had wanted him to take over the family business. But being a restaurateur was the last thing he wanted to be. Having watched his parents slave over their business for years with little to show for it except broken backs and burn scars was deterrent enough. Luckily, his younger brother had taken the reins. With his degree in business management, there was no doubt in Andrew's mind that Daniel could make his parent's place a successful one.

"I get it. I do. I've been there, but in twenty or thirty years, what's going to matter most to you? That you did what your parents wanted you to do based on their outdated ideology, or that you lived your life the way you wanted to and made a career out of something you loved? I'm not saying it'll be easy because it won't be. Paying for your own education is difficult, but, damn, imagine the adventures you can tell your grandkids about from digging up those bones."

Cece sucked in a quick breath as her eyes roamed over his face. "What about *your* grandkids? What kinds of stories are *you* going to tell them about having been a man who defends criminals?"

ELLA DOMINGUEZ

Her words stung, but he took it in stride. "I don't plan on doing this sort of thing for long," he answered in his defense.

"You don't like being a lawyer?"

"I love it. I wouldn't be doing it if I didn't. I mean, I don't love it right this minute, but this job is only a stepping stone. I plan on using everything I learn here for my eventual job working for a district attorney."

When she cringed, he laughed. His parents had reacted the same way.

"Talk about a thankless job," she shook her head. "And you won't even be making a decent wage."

"Maybe not, but it's not about the money for me. If it was, I'd stick with being a defense attorney or go into corporate law. All that matters is that I'll be doing what I love while, hopefully, bringing justice to those who deserve it. *Those* stories will be worth sharing with my grandkids."

Once again, he had left Cece stunned, and the way she sat staring at him, it was as if no one had ever told her it was okay to want something more for herself. Maybe she was one of those individuals whose parents had sheltered her from the opinions of others for the sake of their own selfish agendas. What a disgusting thought. This beautiful, intelligent woman needed to be encouraged to be her own person, not held down and forced to be something she clearly didn't want to be. That was the sort of thing that made a person bitter and angry in the long run.

As they waited for their meals, the palpable energy between them grew, but her next question took him by surprise.

"Why didn't you give that letter to your boss?"

TINY TEMPTATIONS

"I would've loved to have done that. That prick André would deserve it, too, but I figured Claire would end up suffering her dad's wrath just as much as that asshole. Maybe more. And I'm not that mean."

A small smile quirked her mouth. "That was nice of you. You're going to make a shitty defense attorney. You know that, right?"

"Yeah, probably," he agreed. "But don't tell the boss," he laughed. "You know, that butthole André is engaged. Does Claire know that?"

She fingered the edge of her fork and nodded. "She knows."

"I'm glad to hear that. And why do you think her dad has her working in the basement? Why wouldn't he set her up in a nicer office? It's as if he's trying to keep her down there and away from us evil-men-folk like some sort of twisted modern-day Rapunzel."

She smiled and huffed. "I didn't think of it that way, but yeah, you're probably right. He claims he's making her *pay her dues* with the firm."

"Why, is she in law school, too?" he asked with disbelief. Cece nodded. "Holy shit, how many students work in that department?" When she didn't answer, he continued with his inquiry. "Is she anything like her dad?"

"Not even. She's *nothing* like him."

When she stood and walked toward the jukebox at the far end of the diner, Andrew followed behind her and continued with his inquiry.

"Does she look like him?"

She rolled her eyes and let out a loud sigh as she reached into her pocket and dropped several coins into the slot.

"Some people say she has his eyes, but I don't see it."

Realizing he was being rude by talking about another woman, and prompted by Cece's change in mood, Andrew changed the subject.

"Enough about her. Let's talk about you."

She flipped through the selections of albums while shifting from foot to foot "There's nothing to talk about."

He doubted that. Though young, he was fairly positive she had a few interesting stories to tell— probably more interesting than his. He'd love to find out more about her, but she wore her defensiveness on her sleeve, and the chip on her shoulder was pretty obvious. Or maybe that was all just a show. He hoped it was.

"What do you think of him?" she asked.

She punched several buttons causing the carousel to spin, and a Eurythmics tune began playing, drowning out the sounds of the busy Friday night traffic outside.

"André? I already told you …"

"Not him; your boss," she cut in.

When she made her second choice, *I Guess That's Why They Call it the Blues,* he asked, "What are you feeling blue about?"

"Life. Love. Bad decisions in general," she said softly.

"We all make 'em, Kiddo. Love sucks, and this is a bad time of year to reflect on that bullshit."

She nudged him in the ribs with her elbow. "Stop calling me that. I'm only a few years younger than you."

"You have no idea how old I am," he retorted.

TINY TEMPTATIONS

"Well, you alluded to being right out of school, so you can't be more than twenty-five or twenty-six."

"Good deductive skills. You would have made a great lawyer."

Her gaze fixed on him. "Would have?"

"If you hadn't decided to become a paleontologist."

Her smile returned, kindling a fire deep in his belly. It seemed to have that effect on him every time. It was a peculiar thing considering he'd just met her.

"To answer your question: I hardly know Mr. Carlyle. I don't even work directly with him. And he's too busy to deal with us lowly, bottom-of-the-ladder attorneys to get a bead on him. When he interviewed me, I got the impression he's a by-the-book kind of guy—a real taskmaster. I've been told as much, too. What do *you* think of him?"

She pressed a few more buttons to make her final selection of *That's All* and stared up at him. "He's a real hard ass with major control issues. Not just at work, but at home."

"Claire told you that?"

She blinked several times before nodding.

"Damn. I'm glad I didn't give that letter to him."

"Me too, Superman."

F#CK YOU VALENTINE! CHAPTER FOUR

"That was a terrible movie. I can't believe you've paid to see it three times. *And* paid for me to see it."

Cece's statement made Andrew laugh. He had talked her into going to see *Hot Dog* with him though it had hardly taken any effort on his part.

"Just wait, it's going to end up being a cult classic like *The Blob*."

She shook her head. "Another horrible movie."

"You speak blasphemy!" he raised his voice, making her giggle.

"What color was your Pinto?"

Her question came out of nowhere, but he was happy to share the details. "The official name was 'Green Glow.' Why do you ask?"

"I just wanted to get a mental picture of what Clark Kent drove to college."

When they came to rest at a stoplight, she reached into her glove compartment, pulled out a mixtape and slid it into the deck. *Maneater* began a quarter of the way through, and she commenced singing along with it.

"Are you trying to tell me something?" he asked above the loud music.

She simply laughed.

Immediately following the end of the song, and just as they pulled into the empty parking lot of the firm, *Girls on Film* began to play. Parked, she gave him a sheepish grin and even in the darkness, it was easy to see her flushed cheeks.

"This song reminds me that I have an extra ticket to a concert tomorrow," she mentioned casually as she reached over and lowered the music, "and … well …," she trailed off.

He faked shock. "Are you asking me out on a date? Oh, my. Such a progressive girl."

She rolled her eyes and shook her head at his lame joke. "It's Duran Duran at the Arena." Her piercing green eyes bore into him. "I mean, unless you have plans with someone else," she whispered as she picked at the hem of her sweater.

"I don't, but I feel a little bad. I heard those tickets were hard to come by. Maybe you should take a friend or something."

Her lips parted in a soft sigh before responding. "I had planned on taking a college friend, but she backed out. Anyway, I only have one extra ticket, and there'd be a cat fight between my other girlfriends if I chose only one of them. I just figured since we sort of hit if off that … maybe," she shook her head. "Never mind. I understand."

They had hit it off. And frankly, a girl asking him on a date was something new and not at all undesirable. "I didn't say I wouldn't go. Hell, I'd love to go with you." Her somber mood immediately brightened. "But, I'll drive this time," he added.

Her eyes widened with exaggeration. "Not the Green Glow Pinto?"

A short burst of amusement exploded from him. "No, Cece, not the Pinto. I've upgraded to a Toyota Corolla."

"Two or four doors?" she asked with a serious look on her face.

"Four."

The dashboard lights glowed all around her face, highlighting her feminine features and the sensual smile hanging on her lips. "Wow. That's so unbelievably sexy. You really are like Clark Kent, you know?"

"In no one else's eyes except yours, Kiddo."

Although Andrew doubted Cece had any clue as to the power she held, acute awareness of her sexual appeal washed over him, and a deep hunger for the thing he'd been missing in his life stirred in his midsection. Despite the heated look she was throwing his way, he quickly reminded himself to take a chill pill. It was only a concert, for fuck's sake.

***

The loud, almost deafening music pumped all around Cece and Andrew. With sweat-drenched bodies pressed together and hair in their eyes, they danced in the middle of a large crowd as if no one else existed. The seats that must have cost a fortune were some of the best in the arena, but the view of the stage didn't compare to the one next to him.

Cece was stunning in her element. An off-the-shoulder, crop top accentuated all the right parts of her body and her tight jeans left little to the imagination. With her neon blue eye shadow and mascara smudged all around her closed eyes, her cherry lipstick flawlessly in place, her body swaying in time with *The Reflex,* Andrew couldn't think of any other place he'd rather be than there, with her.

When the music broke just long enough for the last song to begin, he leaned down, pulled her close and whisper-yelled into her ear, "You're fucking beautiful."

TINY TEMPTATIONS

The moment *New Moon on Monday* fired up she tugged him down to her level, thrust her hands into his hair and drew his mouth to hers. Clamping her face with his large hands, he brushed his lips back and forth over hers before he exploited her mouth for all its worth. Long, slow kisses that clouded his mind followed next, while the deep bass and synthesizer riffs shook the floor beneath them. Still writhing to the music, their tongues matched their tempo and danced inside each other's mouths, twisting and swirling. Sweeping her up, she wrapped her legs around his waist and gripped his shoulders, their lips never leaving one another's. He traced a path with his mouth and tongue from her mouth to her neck, placing soft, wet, bites to her exposed collar bone. She tasted just as good as she looked, and he made love to her mouth, letting her know how he would make love to her body later.

He'd never wanted an encore to end more than the one playing, but the song couldn't have been more appropriate: *Hungry Like the Wolf.*

Afterwards, the rush of the crowd to get back to their cars was endless, but they were oblivious. Their hands were all over each other and gravity sent all the blood from his head to pool in his groin, making his walk back to his car more than a little uncomfortable.

When they finally reached his vehicle, he opened her door, but not before tugging her close one last time to press his mouth against her neck. The rapid pulse at her throat beat in tempo against his lips and matched his own.

"How about we go back to my place so we can hit a home run?" he whispered in her ear as he caught her lobe between his teeth.

She gently pushed against his chest and gave him a look of incredulity. "*Home run?* No one talks like that anymore." She swallowed loudly. "I want to, but," she paused as uncertainty drew her brows together. "I need to tell you something, but I'm afraid you're going to freak out."

His stomach dropped and the moment of misplaced lust left him shaken. He took a step back. "You have a boyfriend?"

She shook her head, and a look of offense made her body stiffen. "God, no. I wouldn't be here with you if I did."

The silence stretched between them and the yelp of an excited group of women somewhere amidst the crowded parking lot momentarily captured their attention. When their gazes met again, she offered him a nervous smile.

"I really like you. Like, *really really* like you and ..."

He moved close to her again. "Why the hell would I freak out about that?" With his hands wrapped around her waist, he caressed her back and the imprint of her body aligned against his sent frissons of heat along his torso. "Anyway," he flashed his best grin, "what's not to like?"

She reached a hand up to drag a fingertip along his lower lip. "I don't want to rush this."

He sighed with disappointment and shrugged his shoulders. "Okay," he uttered on an exhale. In a flash, his resignation turned to orneriness, and he smiled down at her while waggling his brows. "How about third base?"

A look of surprise left her mouth hanging open.

"Did you really expect me to give up so easily?" he managed to say in between laughs.

TINY TEMPTATIONS

"No. I don't know. Maybe? I'm just shocked. I can't decide if you're too good to be true or if I'm just making this all up in my head."

"Stop over-thinking things, Kiddo. I'm in no rush, even if my hard-on is telling you something else."

***

Despite what Cece had said about not wanting to rush things, they had already made it to second base during the drive back to her place. Her purposeful yet random touches were driving Andrew crazy.

Once parked outside her apartment building—a heated make-out session quickly ensued.

Reaching across her body, he found the lever to the seat, and in one swift motion, it came crashing down causing her to giggle wildly. His heart rate accelerated, and his pulse spiked when she pulled him down against her body to nibble at his lower lip. When she released his lips, he changed the angle of his head, and reclaimed her mouth in a scorching, tonsil-probing kiss that left her breathless. Her back arched, wordlessly asking for more. And so he gave her more.

Send Me an Angel softly playing on the radio, the scent of sweat, cologne and perfume, and soft, guttural moans and wet kisses left Andrew feeling intoxicated.

Somewhere rounding third base, a fire ignited in him for release and a groan rumbled in his throat. Cece must have sensed his need because she pushed against his chest and reached a hand between them to unbutton his jeans and free his shaft from his pants. Her impulsive reaction tore at his resolve. Held captive in that car by her lithe body and sultry voice whispering his name, he was unable to resist pushing the fabric of her shirt up to palm a breast as her fingers encircled his rigid flesh.

She stroked him, slowly, then rapidly, making the base of his spine tingle. Cupping her breasts, he leaned down and sucked and licked at the pink buds of her nipples. Manipulation after sensuous manipulation, his end drew near. Her hand closed tighter around his erection, circling him, tracing each vein and grasping his balls. It was his undoing. With a grunt and jerk, he released onto her stomach and crashed back into his seat. Ragged, quick breaths slowed as he stared up at the pinpricks of stars and bright moon barely shining through the steamed windows.

Realizing the messy predicament he'd left Cece in, he gathered something from the glove box to help her clean up.

When he met her gaze again, he growled, "I'd love to return the favor sometime."

TINY TEMPTATIONS
F#CK YOU VALENTINE! CHAPTER FIVE

After parting ways on Cece's doorstep, they had spent Saturday night talking on the phone until nearly two a.m. Their conversation consisted of everything from his days in South Central New York City living in a cramped two-bedroom apartment with his brother and parents to his college days at NYU cavorting with over-privileged assholes while trying to maintain a 4.0 average.

In turn, she shared a few of her experiences. She'd been an only child growing up in Dallas, and he'd been correct in his assumption that she'd lived a sheltered life. From the looks *and* sounds of it, she had grown up in a wealthy home, though he doubted anyone could tell by her carefree and spirited demeanor. That is, when she wasn't putting up a phony persona and wall of defense like she had when he'd first met her.

Based on his experience, people raised with money were one of two kinds: uptight, arrogant and pretentious, or carelessly-to-dangerously impetuous and without empathy. Cece was neither. At least so far. He hoped, *prayed,* she wasn't putting up a façade.

He tended to see things through rose-colored glasses when it came to romance—something he was painfully aware of. It was one of the reasons he had tried to avoid relationships post Janie Meyers. But, now, with college behind him and his career laid out before him, he had time to dedicate to a relationship, and maybe, *just maybe*, if the stars aligned right, that would happen sooner rather than later.

The time to *return the favor* turned out to be Sunday afternoon. And evening. And night. The entire day had been spent with Cece. Early in the a.m., she'd taken it upon herself to show him the finer points of Dallas, while they intermittently stopped for quick make-out sessions throughout the afternoon. She really knew her stuff—in both regards: Dallas *and* how to wield her tongue inside his mouth.

With the warm sun beating down on his brow, a winter breeze cooling his skin, and Cece's warm hand in his, Andrew allowed himself a moment of contentment. Those didn't come often, so he took advantage of the gift that'd been given to him. He wondered if Cece had any idea just how cherished her company was.

He had learned early on that when something needed to be said—it should be. Having lost several extended family members over the years had taught him there was no time like the present to state your feelings because you may not get the chance again. Sure, it was sentimental and romantic, but he didn't care. Not at the moment anyway. He might feel differently tomorrow, but for now, he was going with the flow.

It occurred to him that the same mentality had gotten him into trouble with Janie. But that was then, and Cece wasn't Janie, nor would he allow himself to compare the two. He hoped Cece was giving him the same benefit of the doubt that he was giving her.

As she stared up at Reunion Tower, he tugged her hand, bringing her full attention to him. "This weekend has been fucking amazing. *You've* been fucking amazing. I know we've just met, but maybe we can see each other again?"

He shook his head. In his own ears he sounded like a wishy-washy pussy, so he could only imagine what he sounded like to Cece. But he felt anything but. He knew for damned sure that he had to see her again, and there was no *maybe* about it.

"Let me rephrase," he said as he pulled her close to stare directly into her eyes while dragging the pad of his thumb across her lower lip. "I *have* to see you again. I *need* to see you again. And I *will*, won't I?" The way he spoke, his decisive tone and the fierceness in his eyes, made his question not so much a request as it was a statement of fact. And judging by the way Cece melted under his gaze and the languid look in her eyes, she understood.

The midday sun cast shadows across her face and emphasized her cherry-red lips when she whispered, "Yes, you will."

Her words reassured him, but the smile she gave him conveyed joy, sadness, and something else he couldn't decipher, and he didn't dare try to figure it out. It was too soon for that.

***

Back at his place and happy to have returned the favor for the third time that day, Cece's taste was still on Andrew's tongue as they sat curled next to each other on his couch.

Her elated mood quickly changed and she stared up at him with a look of sudden panic. Her eyes darted between each of his irises and she stammered, "I'm ... I ... "

The frantic look on her face prompted him to gently prod her. "What is it?"

She gave a gentle shake of her head as if trying to convince herself to do or say something that was difficult. "I hate law school. I'm tired of living here and by my parent's rules. I want *more*. And I want to tell you," she paused as she clutched his forearm, "I just *really* like you and ..."

Taking her face into his hands, he spoke softly. "Then go and get more for yourself. No one can stop you from doing that except you."

Her lips parted as if she had more to add, but she only stared at him.

"Look, Kiddo, I'm not saying I *want* you to leave. Hell, we just met, and I *really* like you too, but you're clearly unhappy. Anyhow, I don't have any ties here, and in a few years, I'm headed out and on to, hopefully, bigger and better things, as well."

"Why couldn't we have met sooner and somewhere else?" she asked sadly.

"We weren't looking. It was the letter that brought us together. I guess we should thank the person who wrote it. And the mailroom for their fuck-up. The next time you work with Claire, tell her I'm sorry about what a douchebag André was to her, but thanks."

Cece stood and walked to the window. With the blinds pushed aside, she stared out at the dismal view of the parking garage.

"Have you ever been in love?"

Her softly spoken question left Andrew temporarily bewildered. They barely knew each other and to be having a conversation about something so intensely personal was more than a little awkward. When she gave him a nervous glance over her shoulder as if mortified with herself, he saw in her what he saw in himself: someone afraid of being hurt yet still willing to keep trying to find the thing that makes people act impetuously—the very thing that made life worth living.

When he realized her question had been a courageous one, he forced himself to answer her, despite his own discomfort. With four long strides, he was standing behind her, his arms wrapped around her waist and his mouth pressed to the nape of her neck, rewarding her for her bravery.

"I thought I was at one time, but I know now it wasn't love. I was young and ..."

"You can be young and in love," she cut in.

"That may be true for some, I suppose. But for me, I was too immature to understand what true love entailed. Even now, I only know what people have told me or what I've seen in other couples. Shit, I don't know any more about love than probably you do. I just know that when I think back about how I felt and the way that girl treated me, I realize I wasn't asking her to love me, I was just seeking her approval." He gripped her shoulders and turned her to face him. "What about you?"

She shook her head and smiled. "The closest I ever came to love was the guy who took my virginity my senior year in high school. He ended up fooling around with one of my so-called-friends, and that fixed my case of school-girl-infatuation real quick." She moistened her lips and stared down at her toes. "There have been a few other men, but nothing ever seems to work out. And it doesn't help that my dad tends to scare off most guys."

"Oh, shit," his voice lowered. "One of *those* dads?"

Her eyes darted to his, and when she saw his playful smile, she giggled. "Yup. One of *those.*"

ELLA DOMINGUEZ

Andrew puffed his chest out in his best imitation of the Man of Steel. "Well, I don't scare easily."

"That's what you say *now.*"

"I'm a lawyer working for a prominent firm, trust me—he'll be impressed," he said as he began to laugh. "Just don't tell him how much I make or the area of town I live in."

Rebellious determination flashed in her eyes like a neon sign. It was damned good look on her.

"I don't care about any of that. And as far as what other people think, including my parents, I don't care about that, either."

Her heated gaze flicked over his body and settled on his chest. Her fingers drew imaginary circles along his well-defined biceps and pecs hidden beneath his shirt. Through her thick lashes, she peeked up at him and grinned as she pulled his concert t-shirt over his head. She reached down and unbuttoned his jeans with skill and tugged them down around his hips.

"Maybe it's the paleontologist in me," she took hold of his rapidly swelling cock and lowered herself to her knees, "but, hot damn, I love searching for the hidden bone."

Cece's warm, wet mouth. Her tongue dancing on the head of his shaft and lapping at his balls. Her tight throat closing around the length of him. Her dark hair shrouding her radiant green eyes and the scent of jasmine and soap. The thick beat of awareness pumping through his veins when her eyes met his.

Each of Andrew's senses was being tempted and teased as Cece's head bobbed up and down lengthwise. When her hands encircled him and twisted in opposite directions milking him of his climax, it was all he could do not to wrench her up by her shoulders and march her to his bedroom to ravage her body.

How long would he have to wait for her? *As long as she required.*

The little lick and suck session had left him sexually frustrated yet oddly satisfied. With the promise of seeing her the following day after work, he'd sent Cece on her way. He had no other choice. He had a brief to file if he was going to keep his job.

F#CK YOU VALENTINE! CHAPTER SIX

Andrew exited the office building to a blast of chilly winter air. Not cold enough for frost, the Texas wind still managed to bite into his flesh. It was early evening and the night sky was just starting to darken. When he stared out at the clouds on the horizon, anxiousness to see Cece's smile again coursed through his veins.

He'd been thinking about her all day, but his busy schedule and a preliminary hearing had prevented him from spending any time with her. It made no difference because she had managed to find a way to be with him. Like a flashback from the good/not-so-good ol' days of junior high, she'd sent him several notes via interdepartmental mail.

All of those letters were tucked into his pocket and the words on them, still etched in his brain: sweet words that expressed excitement to see him again; sincere sentences expressing how much she enjoyed spending the weekend with him; heartfelt paragraphs that conveyed her yearning to taste him again.

His cynicism for the holiday-that-should-not-be-named and everything it represented was no match for the things typed on those two pages. The feeling of being overwhelmed by an all-consuming longing to claim Cece as his own was creeping up on him, and fast. And it had only been a handful of days since meeting her. Just imagine if they were to pursue a relationship? What would become of him then? A blathering, lust-struck idiot like before? He hoped it was a good look on him because he doubted there was much he could do about it at this point.

TINY TEMPTATIONS

Just when he began to chastise himself for acting so foolishly over a girl he hardly knew, he saw her, waiting by his car, and everything he was going to try to convince himself not to feel came rushing back.

Standing with her hands in her coat pocket, she had a peculiar look on her face.

When their gazes met, her eyes lit up like torches. "I have a big day tomorrow."

He brushed his lips against her forehead and inhaled deeply to savor her scent. "Yeah? A big test or something?" he asked as he swept away the hair that had blown into her face.

She thought about his question for a moment before nodding slowly. "Yeah, a *test*."

"Well, then, let's celebrate tonight in anticipation of you doing well," he commented with a wink. When he reached for his car door, she placed her hand over his.

"The only kind of celebrating I want to do is to hit a home run with you."

Andrew's eyes zoomed in on her mouth. He wasn't sure if she was joking, but by the look of desire passing over her features, she was dead serious. Dead *fucking* serious, to be exact. But there was something about her demeanor that seemed odd. *Apprehension*? No. But *something*.

"I thought you didn't want to rush things?" he inquired despite his cock telling him to keep his beerhole shut and take her up on her offer.

"You told me if I wanted *more,* to go and get it. That's what I'm doing. I want *more,* Andrew. Give me *more.*"

The four letter word spoken in a whisper carried the sentiment of a thousand, and the O shape of her shiny red lips when they caressed the syllables sent a rush of blood between his legs. If it was *more* that she wanted, he would give it to her. And then some.

***

A trail of clothes leading to the bedroom. Hands and limbs intertwined and fighting for an inch of flesh. Sheets pulled back. Skin on skin. The snap of a condom and the wet sounds of penetration. Mouths and teeth clashing. Guttural moans and excited groans.

Andrew pushed Cece's knees to her chest and thrust deeply into her until he felt resistance, making her cry out and claw at his shoulders. The taste and the scent of her sex, and his name on her lips—he tried to stay lucid, but it was hopeless. His mind was a mixture of arousal and pleasant confusion at the effect Cece was having on him. Everything about this, about her, was *so* good. *Too. Damned. Good.*

A flip and an adjustment later and he was behind her, *in* her, pumping, her body meeting him thrust for thrust. *So. Damned. Beautiful.* Another flip and he maneuvered her body over his. His hands cupped her ass to lift her high on his cock as she slammed back down onto him. When his thumb circled around her clit, her gaze became riveted on him and she sunk her teeth into her lower lip. The smile and long moan that followed reflected pure contented satisfaction as she achieved release. *So. Fucking. Amazing.*

She quickly dismounted him and in an instant, her head was between his legs. The snap of the rubber could barely be heard over a continuous stream of The Police playing on vinyl in the background. When her mouth engulfed him and her tight, wet throat clutched his shaft, pinpoints of lights detonated behind his closed lids, and with a jerk and a sigh ending in a grunt, he came.

It was all *Too. Damned. Much.* And he wanted *So. Much. More.*

***

Mentally exhausted from work and physically exhausted from enjoying his *home run* with Cece, Andrew had fallen asleep.

The same music that was playing during their bang-fest was still cycling through when he woke to the smell of something sweet. For a split second, he was transported back to NYC and the tiny apartment he'd grown up in.

He rose, dressed in sweat pants, and followed the aroma.

In the kitchen stood Cece, hair pulled up in a messy, high ponytail and another off-the-shoulder top that looked to have been cut from an old sweatshirt. Other than the shirt, she wore only panties. He stood back and watched for nearly a minute as she swayed to the rhythm to *Don't Stand So Close to Me* before he couldn't resist any longer, and spun her around to startle her with a hard, wet kiss.

When they came up for air, he plucked at the fabric of her shirt. "How very *Flashdance* of you."

"Don't be jealous that I'm more fashionable than you," she intoned with a hint of sarcasm.

He peeked over her shoulder. "That smells an awful lot like one of my mother's concoctions."

"I guess that means I did something right. I wasn't sure about some of the measurements, so I winged it. I was looking for a pot to cook in and found a few recipes in one of your unpacked boxes. This one sounded good, so I ran to the store for the ingredients."

She'd found his mother's recipe for English scones. He hadn't had them in nearly two years, and his salivary glands kicked into high gear.

"My mom would be pissed if she knew I'd stolen that recipe from her. They're a hit in my parent's restaurant, and she guards it with her life."

"I won't tell if you don't."

"Thanks for having my back," he mumbled as he coated his finger with a bit of the caramel glaze and dipped it into his mouth. "Hmm, this is different."

Cece turned to face him. "Sorry about that. The recipe for the sauce looked a little out of my cooking league, so I just bought a jar of caramel."

Her apologetic smile and bat of her lashes made it impossible to be disappointed.

"Good effort, Cece," he leaned down to press his lips to her. "And your effort is appreciated more than you know."

Her lips twitched in a rare, intimate smile. "Next time, I'll do it right."

It seemed Cece had a repertoire of smiles for every occasion. This one hinted at the promise of *more.*

Next time: two words that carried the sentiment that *more* than a thousand ever could. Andrew knew in a split second what was so appealing about this woman: *everything*.

TINY TEMPTATIONS

Dazed in the pleasure of Cece's beautiful smile, the mixed scents of her unique perfume and his mother's recipe, and the lull of her voice humming to the music as she placed pink heart sprinkles on the scones, Andrew's world narrowed to nothing but that moment.

Yes, there would definitely be a *next time*.

ELLA DOMINGUEZ

F#CK YOU VALENTINE! CHAPTER SEVEN

After having slept next to Cece the previous night, a strange and almost imperceptible tremor ran along Andrew's nerves when she left early that morning. Perhaps it was the look on her face when he'd wished her good luck with her big test. The *something* that'd felt odd about her demeanor the previous day was still gnawing at him, and even more so now.

He wrote it off as mounting excitement and dread for the holiday that was now upon him. To his shock, he felt the sudden urge to do something about it. Flowers? *Fuck that*. Chocolates? *To hell with that*. Stuffed anim … he stifled the thought as he silently screamed *hell fucking no*. Surely, an educated man such as himself could come up with something more creative than the usual cheap tricks.

As if divine intervention had stepped in, the perfect gift idea came to him. It would take some work to get it done by that evening, especially considering it was a "holiday," but if he had to take off a few hours from work to make it happen, so be it.

He arrived at work early to get the necessary research done and locate a place for the gift he had in mind. With several numbers copied from the Yellow Pages, he placed the phone calls in order to make everything happen. And hopefully, by days' end.

Several hours into the day, he managed to slip away from his desk to sneak down to the transcription department, but Cece was nowhere to be found. When he remembered that she had a test, he decided to take a long lunch to purchase her gift and take it to be engraved. It was going to cost him a good chunk of change since the man who owned the engraving shop was out for the day and making a special trip back in, but what else was Andrew going to spend his money on? *More* trips to the movies alone?

His lunch excursion had taken longer than anticipated, but envisioning Cece's stunned look when she received his gift kept him motivated. When he returned to the firm, no one seemed to notice his late arrival. Something had clearly happened while he was away as evidenced by the small groups of people gathered around speaking in hushed tones. Not one for gossip, Andrew disappeared into his office to stash Cece's gift away in his desk drawer.

Just as Andrew broke out a case file, André peeked in. The stench of his obnoxious cologne immediately put Andrew in a foul mood. Presumably still on his romantic getaway, André had been absent the day before, and his lack of presence had made for a much more peaceful and drama-free work environment.

"Did you hear what happened?"

André knew damn well he hadn't heard what happened and his stupid-ass-question grated on Andrew's nerves. He kept his eyes focused on his work and simply shook his head. To his horror, André stepped into his office and closed the door behind him.

"The old man's daughter quit. Not just her job here, but school. She and Carlyle had a huge blow out in his office. Everyone up on the fourth floor could hear it."

Andrew's eyes drifted upward, but he said nothing. Instead, he clenched his jaw while barely withholding the urge to rip into him for coming into his personal space uninvited. He gave André a pointed stare that should have told him to shut the fuck up and get out of his office, but it went unnoticed.

"She wants to dig up bones!" André belted out a humorless laugh.

All the blood drained from Andrew's face and his vision blurred. "What did you say?" he whispered.

"That bitch wants to dig up bones instead of being a lawyer. Can you fuckin' believe that shit? Of all the ridiculous ..."

Everything else André said was drowned out by the rush of blood and rapidly beating pulse in Andrew's ears.

Claire was Cece? *No*, Cece was Claire. A crimson haze clouded his vision when he realized she, Claire, Cece, whatever-the-fuck, had been lying to him since the very beginning. Anger and hurt pounded and rippled in time to the beat of his heart. The heart that, only moments before, he'd been willing to offer up. A wave of nausea washed over him and his hearing suddenly came rushing back.

"I say good riddance. She was nothing but a tease anyway. Kept me hanging on for damn-near three weeks and never put out," he heard André grumble through the buzz in his ears.

In an instant, Andrew was on his feet as his fist slammed down onto the desk. "Shut the fuck up!" he growled, making André jump with his sudden outburst of rage.

André backed up several steps and gripped the doorknob. "What the hell is your deal?"

Low and deep, his tone belied his true emotions. "You're my fucking deal. You're nothing but a lying, cheating asshole, and if you hadn't been trying to fuck around with Cece she never would've written that damned letter, and I never would've been compelled to return it to her!"

Confusion flashed in André's eyes, only pissing Andrew off further.

"Don't you have any sense of honor?" His voice dropped to a lethal level. "You tried to cheat on your fiancée, lied to Cece ... *Claire*," he corrected himself, "and you have the gall to talk about her that way? You unbelievable ... "

Seething, his statement went unfinished. He stepped around the desk ready to lunge at André and deliver a roundhouse punch to his disrespectful, misogynistic mouth followed by a kick to his *tiny dick* in hopes of stopping his ability to procreate right at the source, but André's sense of fight or flight kicked in, and he flung the door open. Several people outside of Andrew's office window peered in, causing him to glare angrily at them. Once they all scattered, André opened his mouth in rebuttal, but the growl that rumbled in Andrew's throat was enough to make him tuck tail and scurry away.

With the reason for his fucked up situation out of his office, Andrew cleared off his desk in one quick motion. Papers lay strewn everywhere, and adrenaline still pumped through his veins, but he forced himself into his office chair and leaned his head back. With eyes closed, he tried to forget the image of Cece's smile and get his emotions under control.

Nearly fifteen minutes had passed before he finally convinced himself to clean up the mess he'd made. With everything picked up off the floor and placed back on his desk, an interdepartmental envelope caught his attention. When he inspected it, he immediately recognized Cece's distinctive handwriting.

As he scrutinized her handwriting, he tried to recall what the handwriting on André's letter had looked like, but he'd already blocked it from his mind. He had no reason to file something like that away. Once he'd handed the letter to Cece, or rather, *Claire,* he'd pushed it from his mind. There had been more important things to think about, like his budding relationship.

He fingered the envelope and ultimately tossed it aside. He didn't want to read what she had to say.

Forcing his mind to become a blank slate, he cleared his mind of all the drama from the day, slowed his breathing, and focused on his legal case and absolutely nothing else. It was the only way he would get through the rest of the day.

***

With the inevitable end of the work day facing Andrew, he gathered his belongings to leave, including Cece's gift, though he had no idea why or what he would do with it. He glanced around his office one last time before turning the lights off when the manila envelope came into his view. He hovered near the door and stared at it. Before he gave into the curiosity that was gnawing a hole in his gut, he closed the door behind him, and vowed to dispense of it the next day.

When he reached the front reception area, a message was waiting for him. On it was scrawled six words that threatened to tear at his resolve again: *I'll be at Luke's B&B. CC*

TINY TEMPTATIONS

CC, not Cece as he had imagined. *Claire. Fucking. Carlyle.* Her initials were a dead giveaway. Of course, hindsight was 20/20. If only he'd asked for her last name, or for her to spell her first name, he might have figured this all out sooner. Not that asking her for either would have mattered. She probably would've lied about that, too.

He stared at the note for a moment before deciding on what to do. To turn and walk away from this whole situation and never look back was tempting, but that would be taking the easy route, and there was nothing *easy* about this situation. It wouldn't be easy confronting her either, but he deserved answers, even if he didn't want them.

F#CK YOU VALENTINE! CHAPTER EIGHT

Claire had fought the dragon and emerged outwardly unscathed. But she knew the scars of her battle against her father wouldn't show until later. *Much later.*

He'd been swift in cutting off her finances and within a few hours of their showdown, her bank account and credit cards had been frozen. He was callously efficient like that. Luckily, her mother had shown her mercy and offered her some cash to help her land on her feet. It was a surprisingly kind gesture on her mother's part, and one Claire hadn't expected. Even the sadness in her mom's voice and eyes had surprised her. All along she thought her parents were an impenetrable force working hand-in-hand, but the softly spoken words her mother had uttered said otherwise, and now, everything Claire thought she knew about her mom was turning out to be an assumption on her part. It turned out her mother was trapped by her father just as much as she had been. Even worse, her mother was *still* trapped.

But Claire couldn't think about that. She had to get her own life in order before she could help her mother. And she would, too. That much she promised herself.

She stared out the window of Luke's B&B at the gaudy red car her father had purchased for her, and bile rose up in the back of her throat. Undoubtedly he would take that from her, too. It made no difference. She would be happy to be rid of it and the memory of what it represented—her relinquishment of dignity and control.

TINY TEMPTATIONS

Three years of her life had been wasted at that damned school, taking classes she neither cared about nor had a passion for. Three pointless years working in that dank basement *paying her dues.* Twenty-two years under her father's thumb was enough. She was finally free and the one person she wanted to thank for giving her the courage to stand up for herself was nowhere to be seen.

Had he read the letter? She held out hope he had, while praying that he hadn't. It was a confusing situation to be in. She had lied to Andrew and though she believed her reasons were valid at the time, the guilt that had started out as a slow nibble was now consuming her from the inside out.

And all of this on *Valentine's Day*. What a sad, sad joke.

And André-fucking-Heroux. Lying asshole that he was, he'd kept at her, relentlessly trying to weasel his way into her panties for three damned weeks. No matter what he told himself or others, he'd never had a chance. That letter, the root of all this evil, had been written as her final attempt to get him to stop humping her leg like some kind of bitch in heat before she went to her father. A tiny part of her wished she had. But, then she never would have met Andrew— her Superman-in-disguise.

The song that had played over and over while Andrew had made love to her brought her a sense of peace and for a moment, she let the song *Every Breath You Take* playing on the jukebox drown out her anxiety of everything that had transpired that day and what was about to come next.

God, she prayed he showed up. She needed him. And maybe that was pathetic considering she hardly knew him, but she had no one else to go to or who believed in her. His words, his validation, were all she needed to take the next step.

The door to the diner swung open and the chime and cold blast of air that blew in sent goosebumps over her flesh. She smelled Andrew before she saw him—his masculine scent making her lower belly flutter with desire. His hulking, muscular presence was felt next to her and she forced herself to look up into his eyes. They were as indecipherable as his expression. When he combed his fingers through her hair, she nuzzled into his touch.

He hadn't read the letter.

For the briefest of moments, she was relieved. At least for the next few minutes, she could pretend like everything was okay.

Pulling out a chair, he seated himself across from her and placed a brown leather roll adorned with red satin ribbon onto the table and slid it toward her. No man had ever given her a Valentine's Day gift before, and elation filled her heart. She beamed up at him, happy in the moment to keep up the pretense. Like a child on Christmas Day, she frantically tore into her gift, untying the ribbon and loosening the straps at a frenzied pace.

What sat inside the pouch left her breathless and teary-eyed: an engraved rock hammer that read—*Go get more.*

She allowed herself to touch the hammer only once before she swallowed loudly and opened her mouth to confess. But she wasn't quick enough.

"Roses are red. Violets are blue," Andrew began, and at that moment she knew that he knew. "André was a liar," his voice dropped to a husky whisper. "And so are you."

Claire stared into his eyes, unable to find the right words to say. She had already said them all in the letter. With her mouth too dry to speak, Andrew stood and glared down at her.

"Fuck you Valentine. P.S.," he choked out, "I think you can figure out the rest."

When he turned to walk away, she reached out to stop him, but he jerked his hand out of hers.

With her ability to speak suddenly back, she began to plead her case. It was ironic considering she'd just dropped out of law school.

"Please, Andrew. I'm sorry. I wanted to tell you. I tried, but …"

"How much of it was a lie, Cece?" he clenched his jaw. "Correction: *Claire*?"

"None of it," she whispered as she stared up at him. "I mean … I just mean that …"

The words had escaped her again, and Andrew's icy glare was only making matters worse. He had the same look on his face that her father had when he'd forced his rules down her throat, and defensiveness lashed through her.

"I tried to tell you, but you wouldn't let me!"

"You're blaming this on *me?*" he growled.

She quickly backed down. "No, I'm not. I only lied about who I was. Everything I told you about myself and my family was true. All of it. I knew if you found out who my father was, you wouldn't see me anymore."

"*Only* about who you are? Do you even hear yourself? And you're damn straight I wouldn't have pursued you," he retorted as his voice rose several octaves. "I could've lost my job. I can *still* lose my job. We slept together for fuck's sake. Are you so selfish that you can't see what kind of predicament you've put me in? Are you so hell-bent on making your father pay for his mistakes that you're willing to put my career at stake?"

Tears began to leak from her eyes and she was helpless to stop them. "I didn't sleep with you for that reason!"

"When did you plan on telling me who you are? Did you *ever* plan on telling me?"

His words seared through her making the tears unstoppable. Wiping her eyes with the back of her hand, she shook her head as she tried to implore Andrew to hear her out.

"I wrote you a letter telling you everything."

"Today. You wrote that letter *today.* Four damned days too late."

"I always planned on telling you, Andrew. I promise. And you said you didn't scare easily. You said …"

His voice dropped in volume again, and the pained expression on his face sent a new wave of angst crashing through her.

"I know what I said. And I *don't* scare easily, but this is my fucking career, Cece. Damn it, *Claire*, whatever-the-fuck. You could have told me last night. You *should* have told me last night. I was already invested in you at that point."

"How would I know that?" her voice cracked over the last word.

His brows slanted inward, and he shook his head as if confused by his own responses. "You should have told me from the start."

"No," she shook her head. "No. I couldn't have or else we would never have been."

"If everything we were was based on a lie, then maybe we never *should* have been."

The hot, heady scent of his cologne, the agony shining in his blazing blue eyes, and his piercing words seared a path through her heart. Without saying anything more, he turned and walked out, and just as quickly as he'd shown up in her life, he was gone.

With nowhere to go, she lingered in the diner, and with each passing minute, the hope that Andrew would come back, slowly dwindled.

As she stared out at the curtain of dark clouds covering the sky, the realization that she could very well be on her own hit her full force. Taking a note from her father's playbook, she found the fortitude to dry her tears and rise. He may not have been an ideal father or husband, but he had taught her to be strong in the face of adversity. It had served her well when facing off with him. What cruel irony. Maybe Andrew would come around and then again, maybe not. All she could do was hold out hope while moving forward.

With her rock hammer in tow, she pushed her shoulders back and let the words that he'd said to her repeat over and over in her mind.

Go. Get. More.

F#ck You Valentine! Chapter Nine

My test was harder than I ever expected, but I passed it with flying colors, and I have you to thank for it. You've helped me in ways you'll never understand and given me the courage to do what I've known I should do all along. I wanted more and I'm going after it. I only hope you can be part of this new journey I'm about to begin.

I know I should be telling you all of this in person, but I can't. I'm too scared and, so, like the coward I've been since we first met, I'll say it in a letter.

I am Claire Carlyle.

The letter to André was written by me, but please understand, there was never anything between us.

I've been told that every once in a while you'll meet someone who takes you by surprise. Until Friday, I had never experienced that. That person was you. Clark Kent in some ways, Superman in so many others—the few short days I've known you have meant the world to me.

I lied about who I was and for that, I'm truly sorry.

It's unforgivable, even if I had my reasons, and yet, I'm asking you to forgive me. All I can offer in return is a promise that I won't ever lie to you again. Perhaps by sharing my reasons, you'll find it in your heart to let this go, so we can move forward, together.

I liked that you didn't know me. I was a nobody and because of that, my father had no influence over your actions. There were no pretenses between us after our first meeting, and by you not knowing who I was, it allowed you to see me for who I truly am, and not simply Aldrich Carlyle's daughter.

TINY TEMPTATIONS

Being "CC" in your eyes is something I can only describe as an emancipation of sorts.

As for the name CC—I chose it on a whim when faced with your determination, but it turned out to be something I've grown to like, and a name I'm choosing to keep. It only seems fitting. A new life. A new beginning. A new name.

I'm free now, <u>truly free</u>, and I'm asking you, despite the fact that we've only just met, to please be part of my new beginning.

Sincerely, CC.

With CC's letter in one hand and the mixtape she had sent along with it playing on a boom box borrowed from someone's cubicle, Andrew's resolve melted into a thousand pieces.

Unable to sleep, he'd found himself back in his office well after 11 p.m., tearing open the envelope to read her words. He almost wished he hadn't, because now it meant he was facing the challenge of working for the man who had made CC's life hell—a woman whom he deeply cared about. But was he willing to risk his career on a weekend fling? He had no idea. He didn't even know if this thing with her would last. He would never know unless he tried, but it was all just *too damned much* to think about.

With his head tossed back, he stared up at the darkened ceiling tiles while listening to the carefully chosen songs she'd recorded for him. Of those songs: the one that had played during their first kiss; a selection of those that had played during the first time they had made love; several Violent Femmes songs;

and topped off with *True, Hard to Say I'm Sorry* and *Hold Me Now.*

How could he resist a woman who had the same cheesy sentimentality he had? He couldn't—not when he recalled the look of utter happiness on her face when he'd presented her with his gift. He wanted to see that smile again. He *needed* to see that smile again and he wanted to be the reason for it.

Before he lost his nerve, he readied himself to face the challenge that lay ahead, gathered her letter and mixtape, and drove to her apartment.

His determination quickly waned when faced with the possibility that she might not take him back. With his hand poised to knock on her door, all of his old fears of rejection came flooding back. She could very well tell him to fuck off. It wouldn't be uncalled for after the way he'd spoken to her and left her crying in that diner. *God, how could he have been so cruel?* Yes, she had lied and yes, those lies had hurt—but to leave her there after what she'd been through with her father? Even if she didn't take him back, he would apologize for his savage behavior.

His heart took over where his body failed, and, as if watching himself from above, he knocked forcefully on her door. Two long minutes passed before he heard her soft voice from the other side of the door.

"Who is it?"

Even through the metal door it was hard to miss the fearfulness in her tone, and his heart ached for her. Whatever she had been through with Mr. Carlyle had shaken her.

"Andrew," he called out.

The rattle of the chain lock and door latch clicking set his nerves ablaze with anxiousness. When she slowly pulled the door halfway open, the same stunned look that was on her face the first day he'd left her in that basement, was back.

On an impulse and without premeditation, he spoke. "Roses are red. Violets are blue. You fucked up, and I did, too."

A smile creased the corners of her lips and tears filled her eyes. More importantly, the fear she'd exuded only moments before seemed to vanish. As did his.

"How about we be fuck-ups together?" he asked.

She reached a hand up to touch his cheek as if making sure he was real.

"I'd love to be your side-fuck. No, wait ...your side-kick-fuck-up," she stammered. "This isn't coming out right at all."

Joy bubbled in her laugh and shone in her eyes as she exhaled and swung the door open fully to allow him in. His gaze fell to the pout of her lower lip as he slid his hand behind her neck to draw her close.

"I'm sorry I left you in the diner, upset. I won't ever do that again."

CC softened under his touch and her eyes fixed on his.

"I'm sorry I lied. I won't ever do that again."

The sexual tension that had been a constant undercurrent between them was ever present, urging him forward. Taking her hands into his, he kissed her knuckles and put everything on the line.

"Do you still want more?"

On a sigh, she wrapped her arms around his waist and pressed her cheek against his chest.

"Yes, Andrew, I want so much more."

Her full-blown Southern drawl washed over him with heat and desire. When he saw the look of surrender on face that said she belonged to him, a deep primal growl rumbled in his throat. It was a damned good look on her. The best one yet. She was his, and even though this thing between them might only last another day or a week, for now, *She. Was. His*. They could figure out the rest later.

He reached a hand up to adjust his glasses on his nose, and flashed his best Clark Kent smile.

With CC swept up into his arms, he kicked the door closed behind him and whispered into her ear, "Let's go get *more*, Kiddo."

TINY TEMPTATIONS

ENGLISH SCONES with SALTED CARAMEL SAUCE

Ingredients:
2 cups (240g) all-purpose flour
2 and 1/2 teaspoons baking powder
½ teaspoon salt
1/2 cup (115g) unsalted butter, frozen
1/2 cup (120ml) heavy cream
1 large egg
1/2 cup (100g) packed light or dark brown sugar
1 teaspoon vanilla extract
optional: 1 Tablespoon cream and coarse sugar
1/2 cup (120ml) caramel sauce (recipe below)

Instructions:
Preheat oven to 400°F (204°C). Adjust baking rack to the middle-low position. Line a large baking sheet with parchment paper. Set aside.

Whisk the flour, baking powder, and salt. Grate the frozen butter via a box grater or food processor. Place grated butter into flour mixture. Combine with a fork or your fingers until the mixture resembles coarse meal. Set aside.

In a separate bowl, whisk the cream, egg, brown sugar, and vanilla together. Drizzle over the flour mixture and then toss the mixture together with a rubber spatula until everything appears moistened. Try not to overwork the dough. Dough will appear slightly wet. Work the dough into a ball with floured hands and transfer to a floured surface. Press into an 8″ disc and cut into 8 equal wedges. Place scones at minimum of 2 inches apart on the prepared baking sheet. Brush scones with optional 1 Tbsp cream and sprinkle with coarse sugar. (Will give them shiny outer shell and add a little extra crunch)

Bake for 20-25 minutes or until lightly golden and cooked through. Allow to cool for a several minutes before drizzling with caramel sauce.

Tip: Scones are best when fresh, but leftovers will keep well at room temperature for 2 extra days. Scones can be frozen for up to 3 months. Thaw overnight in the refrigerator and heat to your desired temperature before eating.

SALTED CARAMEL SAUCE
Ingredients:
1 stick butter (4 ounces)
¾ cup packed light or dark brown sugar (light brown sugar will give the sauce a lighter color)
½ cup whipping or heavy cream
1 teaspoon vanilla extract
Pinch of sea salt

Instructions:
Melt butter in a sauce pan over medium heat. Add brown sugar and whisk to combine.

Add cream. Bring to a boil, then reduce to a low simmer and cook an additional 5 minutes, stirring frequently. Add vanilla and sea salt. Stir until combined.

Serve warm or allow to cool. Stir vigorously, then store in refrigerator. Mixture will thicken as it cools.

♥ **Pink heart sprinkles optional** ♥

TINY TEMPTATIONS
F#CK YOU VALENTINE! EPILOGUE

COMING SOON. Want to be the first to read it? Sign up for Ella D.'s newsletter.

http://eepurl.com/bwsvUf

ELLA DOMINGUEZ

A CUB FOR CHRISTMAS

Copyright © Ella Dominguez, 2015
All Rights Reserved
Bondage Bunny Publishing

TINY TEMPTATIONS
A CUB FOR CHRISTMAS: ACKNOWLEDGEMENTS

A very sincere and appreciative thank you goes out to my beta readers and fans.

ELLA DOMINGUEZ

A CUB FOR CHRISTMAS: PLAYLIST

Only an Older Woman
by The Boy from Oz by **Peter Allen**
Mrs. Robinson by **Simon and Garfunkle**
Friends with Benefits by **Ceann**
My Young Man by **Esmé Patterson**
You Sexy Thing by **Hot Chocolate**
December (based on "September")
by **Earth, Wind & Fire**

TINY TEMPTATIONS
A CUB FOR CHRISTMAS: LONG STORY SHORT

Romantic, sweet and scorching hot.

When a chance meeting at a Broadway show leads to an unexpected attraction, things quickly heat up. With Aaron's hypnotic blue eyes distorting Ari's vision and judgment, the loud traffic buzzing in her ears, his masculine scent filling her nose, his body heat enveloping her and his breath ghosting across her lips, it's only inevitable that she give into the temptation of a younger man. How can she deny the allure when she suddenly feels sensory overloaded and more alive than she's felt in more than a decade?

Set in New York City, the undeniable pull between this May-December romance burns up the pages when Ari realizes that unwrapping her Christmas package is only half the fun.

ELLA DOMINGUEZ

A CUB FOR CHRISTMAS: CHAPTER ONE

A holiday away from the holidays is precisely what Aricelli wanted. More to the point, it's exactly what she needed. With her children spending their winter breaks on the other side of the country with their father, a trip into the city sounded much more festive than being alone in her bungalow.

The smell of expensive cologne and perfume settled all around her as she found her balcony seat. She had almost been late to the show due to traffic, something she was unaccustomed to. The most traffic she ever saw in her small town was during the homecoming parade, and that was nothing compared to Broadway on Friday night. She had barely taken off her wrap when the lights above her blinked and the sounds of voices, violin strings, French horns and the low beat of drums died down to an almost deafening silence.

She loved this part: the anticipation and exhilaration of what was to come next. Perched on the edge of her seat, her nerves tingled. Being alone wasn't something she enjoyed, but if she was going to do it, there was no better place than the New York City Theatre watching The Nutcracker Suite.

An hour later, her heart was still racing from the animation of the play. After a quick trip to the ladies room, she was mingling amongst the other well-dressed theatergoers.

Standing near one of the glass-front windows, the reflection of a tuxedo-wearing man approaching her made her turn away from the busy street view. When she faced him, she was immediately struck at the intensity of his deep-blue eyes. She tried to keep her eyes locked on his face, but they drifted over his body anyway. Holding two glasses of champagne, he offered her one as his eyes flicked to her left hand not once, but twice.

When she accepted his gift, he offered her a polite smile. "Is attending the ballet alone something you do often?"

Her belly fluttered at the way his gaze casually slid down her body before rising to meet hers again.

"No, not often," she brought the glass to her mouth as she gave him a slow, appraising glance.

He was young with cropped, dark wavy hair styled in that just-got-fucked way. He was late twenties at the most, and that was a conservative guess. The solid black tuxedo he'd chosen fit him like a glove and only accentuated the alluring sexuality that seemed to swirl all around him. Yes, he was definitely too young for the thoughts she having about him.

"Just when your husband is away?" His neutral tone did little to disguise the curiosity that throbbed in his voice.

He was adorable, but not very good at subtlety. She flicked him an amused look from beneath her lashes, "Subtlety isn't your strong suit, is it?"

Her soft laughter made him shift uncomfortably from foot to foot. "Right. Sorry," he reached a hand up to rub the back of his neck. "I'm usually better at this."

By *this,* did he mean flirting? *One could hope*. In an attempt to put him at ease and break the awkward silence beginning to build between them, she asked, "What brings you here? Are you dating one of the dancers?"

She cringed at her question. He wasn't the only one terrible at subtlety.

His breathy laugh only added to his charm. "It's a nice break from reality, and I don't date dancers," he readjusted his bowtie. "They're too focused on dancing to see what's right in front of them."

"Are you speaking from experience?" she asked when she saw the smile fade from his eyes and mouth. He shrugged a slow roll of one massive shoulder, leaving her question unanswered. "I wanted to be a dancer, though I suppose every little girl does at some time or another," she whispered half to herself, half to him.

Remembering a time when her dreams for the future were still fresh, she stared at the toes of her shoes. *Where had the years gone*? She didn't have any regrets about the way her life had turned out, other than her divorce, but even that had turned out for the best.

"What stopped you?"

His voice made her want to lean closer to revel his inquisitiveness. Glancing upward, she met his gaze head-on. "Life. Kids. Work." He seemed mesmerized by her, his eyes fixed on her mouth. "And the fact that I can't take one step in front of the other without eventually stumbling over myself. Grace is a hard thing to come by for me."

"Yeah, that might be a problem," his deep laughter rumbled through him. "Anyway, you seem to be doing just fine." His eyes roamed over her body yet again, and the quivering in her belly from only a moment ago returned.

"Give me a few minutes, I'm sure it'll wear off."

TINY TEMPTATIONS

"I doubt that," he shook his head in disbelief. "By the way," he stared down at her with smoldering intensity as he brought the flute of champagne to his lips and peered over the rim, "you smell amazing."

His underlying casual flirtatiousness was captivating. She took it back, he *was* good. And apparently he was regaining his footing in their little cat and mouse game.

"What perfume are you wearing?"

As enjoyable as his attention was, it was time to put an end to this little diversion. Thinking of the least sexy thing she could come back with, she answered, "Dial and deodorant." A questioning look flitted over his rugged yet youthful face. "I'm not wearing any," she clarified.

Once again, he brought his drink to his lips. As if enjoying torturing her with his measured response, he sipped on his drink while staring at her mouth.

"Interesting," he finally answered.

The only thing *interesting* was that she had entertained this conversation as long as she had. He opened his mouth to saying something more, but the hum of the orchestra firing up interrupted him and signaled that their brief intermission was over. Laying down her goblet on a nearby tray, she gave the attractive but far-too-young man a sideways glance.

"Thanks for the drink."

"No, *thank you*," he flashed his million-dollar smile.

She turned to leave, but couldn't fight the urge to take one last look at him. Peering over her shoulder, she found him watching her. Well, not so much her as staring at her ass. Flattered, she gave him her best sensual smile. And why shouldn't she? She would never see him again.

Feeling ambitious, she took it a step further. "By the way, you smell fantastic, as well. And you look amazing in that tux."

She took two steps when he called out to her, "Do you have a name?"

"Of course," she waved over her shoulder. "But let's not ruin the fantasy."

Back in her seat, she couldn't help but scan the crowd for him. His incredible eyes had knocked her for a loop and she wanted just one more look at them.

Unable to find him, she became ensnared in the production once again. The lean bodies of the dancers as they floated around the stage… the familiar music that brought back memories of happier times her when her marriage was still intact and her children young…

Another hour later, the stage lights died down and the dance company gave their final bows. Just as the bright overhead lights came on, she spotted the man who had offered her a drink and renewed her confidence in herself. From the opposing balcony, he gave her a nod and a smile, his gaze so focused on her that for a moment, it held her prisoner.

The crowd momentarily distracted her and when she looked back, he was gone

TINY TEMPTATIONS
A CUB FOR CHRISTMAS: CHAPTER TWO

Back on Broadway with a cold northern wind whipping against her body, Aricelli waited her turn to hail a cab. Only a few minutes passed when she felt a tap on her shoulder.

Turning, she came face-to-face with Blue Eyes.

"It's too early to call it a night. And this wind, Jesus," he braced himself against another blast, "how about we get some hot cocoa?"

Wrapping her arms around herself, she shook her head. "I don't have drinks with strangers."

A lopsided grin curved one side of mouth, "Okay. But, technically, you've already had a drink with me."

He did have a point, though she wasn't about to admit that to him. "That didn't count."

Undeterred, he kept moving right along, "And now you want to exchange names?" The husky rasp of his laugh filled the night air just before he cleared his throat. "Fantasy readjustment time," he straightened up and thrust his hand in her direction, "I'm Aaron."

His charisma was undeniable and his voice like long vowels dipped in finely aged red wine that flowed over her. Unable to resist his charm, she took his hand when he suddenly pulled her close and leaned into her. "And hot chocolate hardly counts as a drink."

Another point well-made. And those eyes... well, how could she deny him? Nodding her agreement, he tucked her into his body for warmth and led the way to an upscale café not far from the theatre.

Once inside, they found a corner table.

Rubbing her hands together for warmth and then breathing into them, she wished she had brought something heavier to wear.

"In case someone forgot to tell you, it's winter," Aaron quickly removed his expensive-looking overcoat and wrapped it around her shoulders.

"Thanks. It was warmer where I came from when I left this afternoon."

His wide eyes reflected surprise. "You're not from the city?"

"No, upstate," she slipped her arms into the sleeves of his coat. "About four hours from here."

"So, tell me: what are you doing alone in the city two days before Christmas? You mentioned kids, where are they?"

"With their father in Oregon."

Like a practiced aristocrat, he pulled his tie loose in one smooth motion and slid it into his pocket.

"Why didn't you join them? I hear Oregon is great this time of year."

Just then the waitress arrived and he was quick to order them both cups of hot chocolate. He glanced at her, "Marshmallows?"

There was an edge of command not only in his actions, like the way he had shielded her against the cold wind and then chivalrously placed his jacket around her, but in his voice. It was the kind of authority that always sent a wave of goosebumps over her flesh. She reminded herself of their age difference before nodding yes to the marshmallows, and sending the waitress on her way.

Staring across the table at her, he waited patiently for her response.

TINY TEMPTATIONS

"Their father and I…," she hesitated a moment, choosing her words carefully as to not sound bitter about the way her marriage had ended. "We're not pals."

Understanding shone in his eyes. "I see."

"So, you tell me," she swiftly changed the subject, "who was the dancer who broke your heart?"

A surprised smile lit up his face, and she could only guess it was from the brazenness of her question. Shaking his head, he answered, "It wasn't like that. My mom was a dancer," he quickly rephrased. "Correction: *is* a dancer. Like she frequently points out: *once a dancer, always a dancer.*"

She couldn't mask the enthusiasm in her voice at the mental image of this handsome man having a beautiful dancer for a mother. "Really? Being raised by a dancer must've been exciting for you."

His crooked smile reappeared. "It was definitely *something*. If anything, it gave me an appreciation for music," he cleared his throat. "What kind of work do you do?"

She slumped into the vinyl seat, disappointed with his abrupt change of subject, even though she had done the same. "I work from home answering calls as a crisis hotline counselor."

"Wow. That must be stressful. And working from home? I wouldn't have the discipline to do that. I'm impressed."

"Stressful yes, but definitely not impressive. I definitely miss the social contact, but it sure feels good when I've helped someone. Anyway, it worked out great when my kids were home. Now that they're gone, cabin fever has started to set in."

"No wonder you ventured out into the city. You needed *stimulation*."

There was no restraint in the suggestive tone of his comment and for a split second, she had the urge to lunge across the table and tear his clothes off to show him exactly what would *stimulate* her. When she felt the blood rise to her cheeks from not only his statement, but her inner thoughts, a faint smirk touched the corners of his lips.

"Well, my job definitely isn't as *arousing* and artistic as dancing, but you're right: I do need *stimulation*."

When she smiled back, her lips presented a temptation that seemed to make him edgy causing him to shift in his seat. A man hadn't looked at her like that in a long time - with genuine interest and unabashed desire. She must be crazy for even allowing the idea of being with him to cross her mind, but her bodily response to him was overwhelming, and when she saw the fierce sparkling in his eyes, her pulse kicked. *He wanted her*. Her nerves danced, her brain raced and her hormones sent a flash of heat that washed over her like a tidal wave.

Silence lingered between them as they assessed each other, and she began to play out the rest of the night in her mind: smiles, more flirting, casual touches. And if she was feeling really adventurous, drinks back at his place or even at her hotel room.

Just then their cocoa arrived and once again, he took charge as he slid her cup toward him to stir it and add a few ice cubes from his water glass to cool it down for her.

Trying to resist the sweet pull of desire building between them, she resorted to casual conversation.

TINY TEMPTATIONS

"What does a handsome young man like yourself do to earn a paycheck?"

His body grew still as his irises flicked from her eyes to her mouth. After a short pause, he answered, "I work two jobs: as a mail clerk and waiter," he smoothed his palm over one lapel of his tux. "My friend gave me his ticket to the show and loaned me the tux and coat for the night."

She considered his response while recalling what it was like to be young and struggling financially. "That's some friend," she smiled. "You work two jobs and yet you made time to go to the ballet. That sounds like some kind of Christmas miracle."

His brows slanted inward, his lips parting as if wanting to say something more. Licking his lips, he averted his eyes to the tabletop and fidgeted with the flatware on the table. She was unable to distinguish whether he was momentarily suffering from a sudden loss of confidence or just nervousness, but regardless, it was upsetting to see. If he was worried about her not liking him because he wasn't well off, he had her pegged all wrong. Frankly, she could care less. He had been nothing but a gentleman all evening and that alone meant more to her than the amount of money he did or did not have in his bank account.

Trying to put him at ease, she reached across the table to touch the top of his hand. "Thanks for inviting me out. I had planned on just crashing at my hotel, but this is far more pleasurable."

His self-assurance returned full force. "You're something else, you know that?"

Maybe she was. Then again, maybe she was just grateful that he had reminded her that she was still attractive. Whatever the case may be, she made the conscious decision to enjoy her allotted time with him, even if he hadn't asked her name.

Another hour passed before Aricelli realized how late it was. Hating to be the one to break the bad news, she pointed out that she had to be up early for her drive back home.

Back out on the street, she took off his coat, but when she tried to return it, he gently pushed it toward her.

"You keep it. You need it more than I do."

"You're sweet, and I appreciate the gesture, but I don't think your friend would want to part with it," she handed it to him.

A look of guilt flashed across his face. Or something. She couldn't tell and he looked and smelled too good to care. She dared to lean into him, putting their unspoken age difference out of her mind. With his hypnotic blue eyes distorting her vision and judgment, the loud traffic buzzing in her ears, his masculine scent filling her nose, his body heat enveloping her and his breath ghosting across her lips, she suddenly felt sensory overloaded, and more alive than she had felt in a decade.

Their mouths had barely touched when he fingered a wisp of hair away from her face and pulled away. "I don't kiss strangers on the first date."

God, that voice - soft and even, and those eyes - infinitely wicked and gleaming with carnal desire… She quickly recovered from her entrancement and met his roguish gaze.

"So, now you want my name?" she mimicked his tone from earlier. "Okay. I'm Aricelli," she thrust her hand toward him. "And that hardly counts as a kiss."

TINY TEMPTATIONS

A Machiavellian-like grin spread across his face. "You're right," he gripped her hand and yanked her toward him. "*This* is a kiss."

With one hand around her neck and the other around her waist, he began a tortuous trail along her jaw line with his tongue and nibbling teeth before he crushed his mouth to hers. There was an unexpected wildness in his taste that was a combination of cocoa and passion. He pulled back only to exert more provocative pressure with his lips as his tongue probed her mouth, swirling around and exploiting her depths. The long, slow kiss that lingered between them clouded her mind until she felt the hard thickness of his shaft press into her belly. His tenderness turned fierce in an instant like he wanted to devour her completely. And she allowed it because that's exactly what she wanted – to be consumed by his toe-curling determination to have her. Just when she thought she would combust from the fire he had rekindled within her, he broke the seal of their kiss, leaving her breathless and wanting more. Gently, he kissed her forehead and reluctantly released her.

She hoped he would suggest they go somewhere, but instead, he waved down a taxi for her and reached into his wallet.

"You have a long drive tomorrow, you need your rest," he sighed miserably as he handed her a business card. "If you're in the city any time soon, give me a call."

As the cab drove away, she glanced back to see him watching her. And then, he was gone. Again.

ELLA DOMINGUEZ

A CUB FOR CHRISTMAS: CHAPTER THREE

Aricelli no sooner made it into her hotel room when she threw herself onto the bed, fully clothed. The chill of the cold night air was still lingering on her skin as was Aaron's scent, making it difficult to think about anything else except that kiss.

She reached into her clutch and pulled out the card he gave her, suddenly finding it odd that a mail clerk/waiter would even carry one. And a very nice one at that. She could tell by the weight of the paper and the script and ink that the cards had cost him a small fortune. If she had learned anything from her time with her ex-husband, it was how to tell *money* when she saw it. Even in the most mundane details. Still too flustered from Aaron's drugging kiss, she dismissed the thought altogether.

After unclothing and climbing into the hot shower, her mind went back to that kiss... his strong arms... the outline of his shaft pressed into her... his light-bronze skin and high cheekbones. When the intensity of his blue eyes penetrated her thoughts, her hands found their way to her breasts and her fingers plucked at her nipples before moving downward to the place where her pleasure was centered.

She closed her eyes and tried to imagine what it would feel like to be with someone like Aaron. No, not *someone* like him, *him.* That perfect mouth of his doing things to her body that she had only fantasized about... his hands seeking out and finding her erogenous zones... his driving thrusts of passion bringing her to the brink of ecstasy. When a cool chill followed by searing heat settled between her legs and

TINY TEMPTATIONS

her lower belly began to shudder, she allowed herself to replay their kiss one last time before she moved on.

*

When she woke in the morning, she felt unexpectedly invigorated. She had dreamt of a beautiful, blue-eyed stranger the night before and even as she dressed and packed, she was finding excuses to stay in the city another night in hopes of another saucy encounter. Staring at the business card that lay on the bathroom counter as she brushed her teeth, she read and reread the name over and over in her mind: *Aaron McAvoy*.

Walking out of the hotel with purpose, she dialed his number before she lost her courage. To her disappointment, she was promptly sent to voicemail. After leaving a message with her number, she stood on the street and stared up at the tall buildings surrounding her while trying to imagine Aaron hard at work, waiting on undeserving restaurant patrons. She hoped they were treating the polite young man kindly.

The streets were packed with traffic and the stores were teeming with pushy last minute shoppers. The 'holiday spirit' was quickly becoming overwhelming, so she ducked into a nearby vintage clothing store to purchase a coat while taking a short break from the hustle and bustle before hailing a cab to take her somewhere to eat.

As she made her way back out to the busy street and into a cab, she briefly considered going to the address listed on the card but figured it was a long shot, and maybe even too presumptuous. However, on second thought, if he was there, it might be worth it. Or maybe not. Perhaps he would rebuff her, though she doubted it. She remembered well the look on his face and how much he seemed to want her.

Just as she was seated by a waitress, her phone rang out. Answering, she heard Aaron's smooth voice on the other end.

"Aricelli...," his baritone voice dripped with surprise.

"I hope I didn't interrupt anything important," she answered, unable to resist smiling at how quickly he had returned her call.

"Not at all. I was hoping you'd call." Though young, he had a voice like aged whiskey.

"It turns out I need to run a few errands while in the city before I leave," she stated, while trying to envision his blue eyes wide with anticipation. "I considered stopping by the address on your card..."

"Oh, no, I'm glad you didn't," he cut in, his tone suddenly revealing nervousness.

"Is something wrong?" she asked.

"No," she could hear him sigh on the other end. "Where are you? Can we meet for lunch?"

"I'd love that. I'm at the Deli Citron."

"I know where it is. Give me about twenty minutes," he paused only a second, but the lazy sensuality of his next statement resonated in a tone that trickled down her spine like warm velvet, "I can't wait to see you."

Twenty minutes passed by in the blink of an eye while she people-watched, and right on time, he walked through the doors of the small deli, his eyes immediately finding hers. She scanned him quickly, thrown off by his wearing yet another posh coat, suit and shoes. For a man who claimed to work two jobs, he sure had expensive tastes.

Her scrutinizing glance didn't go unnoticed by Aaron, though he said nothing.

Sitting down across from her, he took a hold of her hands, and when he rubbed his thumbs over the tops of them, the warmth of his touch and dark gaze seemed to suck the air from her lungs.

Staring into his eyes, she confessed, "You have a strange effect on me."

"Strange?" he quirked his brows in confusion.

"I know I shouldn't be thinking about you the way I am, but…" she didn't know how to convey what she was feeling. Hell, she didn't even know *what* she was feeling other than a deep yearning to sample his goods.

He turned her hand over and began tracing the lines of her palms. "Why shouldn't you be?"

"Your age," the words caught in her throat when she finally stated the obvious.

"You have no idea what my age is," amusement tightened the masculine features of his face when he smiled.

"You can't be more than thirty."

"I'm not," his grin widened. "Does that bother you?"

She slid her hands across the table and placed them in her lap. "I wouldn't be here if it did," she whispered, as she licked her lips as she continued to keep her eyes riveted to his. "But, I'd be lying if I said it wasn't more than just a slight distraction."

He tipped the chair back onto two legs with casual ease. "Are you attracted to me?"

"Obviously."

His unique, throaty laugh sent her belly aflutter again, but his laughter quickly died down as he ran his fingers through his already mussed hair.

"And obviously I'm attracted to you. Age has nothing to do with it," he gave a slight shake of his head as if trying to talk himself into doing something. "There's no time like the present," he stated mysteriously. "I need to tell you something before this goes any further," his eyes darted back to hers and he swallowed tensely. "Well, more like *admit* something."

Oh, God.

Aricelli's stomach dropped. If Aaron admitted that he was married, she could scream. But not before slapping his beautiful chiseled face for leading her on.

"I don't work two jobs," he continued to meet her gaze straight on.

Both stunned and relieved, she sat quietly staring back at him. "Why would you lie about something like that?"

"Because the fact is that…," he seemed to search for the right wording, "I'm worth a sizeable amount." He suddenly seemed embarrassed, "I didn't know what your intentions might be if you knew that."

Irritation kicked in as she crossed her arms over her chest. "I'm not sure what I did to make you question my intentions, but you were the one to hit on me, remember? And in case you hadn't noticed, I'm a grown woman, not some girl who's looking for a man to secure her future or pay her way in life," she reached for her handbag.

"I know that now," he sat forward and brought the chair down onto four legs when she stood.

"Aricelli, wait," his frantic voice called out to her just as she reached the door.

"I don't have time for this," she mumbled just before she felt his hand on her upper arm.

"It was a shitty thing to do, but I didn't think I'd ever see you again."

"You're ridiculous," she tried to escape his stronghold.

"I am. I admit it. But I honestly didn't think you would call," the volume of his voice dropped to a mere whisper.

He spoke with a quiet strength that brought her eyes around to meet his. "If you didn't want me to call you, then why did you give me your card?" she asked, confused by the tight note in his voice that hinted at concern.

His eyes widened. "I *did* want you to call. I just didn't think that you would. I mean, a woman like you..."

"You mean an *older* woman like me?" defensiveness laced her words.

"No, I didn't mean that. I meant...," an exasperated sigh slipped past his lips, "you're just so damned beautiful and put together. I don't usually attract women like that."

Her insides sang at the sincerity of his compliment, but she still wondered... "What kinds of women do you normally attract?"

His eyes zoomed in on the movement of her lips and a shy smile replaced his usual confidence. "We can save that conversation for another day."

With all her being she hated lying, however, when she saw genuine regret staring back at her, she decided to give him just one more chance. She had forgiven others for far worse offenses, including her ex-husband, so surely Aaron deserved another chance. But she wouldn't put up with dishonesty, *ever*. To make her wishes undeniably clear, she narrowed her eyes, reached a hand up, gripped the lapels of his pricey suit jacket and drew him close enough that he could feel her breath on his lips when she spoke.

"Don't lie to me again."

A flash of understanding shone in his eyes when he pressed his body against hers and wrapped an arm around her waist. Swiping a finger across her forehead, he glided it down her jaw and ghosted it over her lips, "Absolutely not."

TINY TEMPTATIONS
A CUB FOR CHRISTMAS: CHAPTER FOUR

Whisking Aricelli out of the deli, Aaron guided her to a black car waiting half a block down. But not just any car, a classic car inside which a man no more than a handful of years older than herself sat waiting. Having attended the Barrett-Jackson car show with her ex-husband eight years standing, she immediately knew what the make and model of the vehicle was. That endeavor had proven educational, even if she had found it boring at the time. But then again, maybe it was just the company she was in.

From that experience, she found that when a person was afforded the opportunity to purchase any car they so desired, what they chose to drive said a lot about them. To her, Aaron's choice said: *understated, yet oddly charming.* She supposed that was true enough from the few conversations she'd had with him and the fact that he had felt the need to come-clean with her before things got hot and heavy. Any other man probably would've just kept up the lie just to save face and/or get in her panties.

Ever the gentleman, he opened the door for her and guided her into the rear seat.

"Nice ride," she commented as she scanned the perfectly restored interior.

"Thanks," he glided his palm over the fabric of the seat.

"Personally, I prefer the '63 Max Wedge Fury over the Valiant," she absent-mindedly whispered as she outlined the red houndstooth design with a fingertip. "If I was a Plymouth person that is, which I'm not."

"You know cars?" His voice hinted at amusement.

"A little."

"Now who's lying?" he nudged her. She smiled up at him and lifted her shoulders in an ironic shrug. Lowering his voice as he bent his head close to hers, he asked, "So, if you're a not a Plymouth gal, then what?"

"Buick."

His mouth twitched at one end into a wry grin when he prodded her further, "Which model?"

The way he was staring at her, expectantly, curiosity brimming in his irises – she had never seen such a look of unadulterated longing directed at her. Those eyes, bottomless and as clear and deep as the Pacific Ocean shimmered with pure sensuality, and were only enhanced by his thick, dark lashes.

She blinked several times trying to formulate a coherent response to his question. "The 1963 Riviera."

"Yeah," his eyes drifted for a moment as if imaging it. "That one's a beauty." He wrapped an arm around her shoulders and tugged at the fabric of her newly-purchased wool coat. "I see you have a taste for the vintage as well," he winked. "Nice choice."

"So," she cleared her throat, "what kind of work does one do that they can afford a completely restored 1962 Plymouth Valiant as a get-away car?"

Again, he appeared impressed at her knowledge. "I helped develop a piece of software with my college roommate five years ago. Some big investors threw some money our way in order to bring it to completion. We've been able to implement it into some pretty useful consumer and government applications."

"Wow. You sound so *grown up,*" she kidded.

TINY TEMPTATIONS

"Oh, God, no. Not *grown up*," he laughed. "More like boring. Sorry. It really is a dull, nerdy business that lacks in sex appeal, but it pays the bills and gives me some play money."

Aaron had sex appeal in spades and he certainly didn't need any help in that department. And she doubted there was anything *dull and nerdy* about him.

"What's the name of your business?" she reached up to straighten his tie.

"Toggle. It's a GPS coordination application that..."

"Yes," she interrupted. "I know what it does. I have it installed on my car's GPS device."

His eyes lit up, "No shit? Nice. I guess our marketing team is doing their job after all."

"Definitely. If you think about it, it was your own ingenuity that brought me here to the city. I would've been lost somewhere in Brooklyn if I hadn't used it."

"That would've been a tragedy," his voice dropped to a husky murmur as he reached a hand up to drag his thumb across her bottom lip. "Damn, you're gorgeous," he said so softly she almost didn't hear him over the buzz of the traffic. "Tonight," he dipped his head down to whisper into her ear. "Will you spend it with me? Dinner, another show, a helicopter ride over the city to see the Christmas lights... whatever you want."

"But it's Christmas Eve. What about your family?"

His brows pinched together, "The only holiday tradition my family practices is avoiding each other."

Steering clear of an obviously touchy subject, Aricelli quickly redirected their conversation. "I do love Broadway shows."

"Me, too. All of them. Even the *ridiculous* ones," he teased.

"You would, being as you *are* ridiculous," she pressed her body flush against his and dragged his manly scent into her lungs. "And I've never been on a helicopter."

"Then, allow me be the first to take you on one, Aricelli…" his voice trailed off as he drew her close and his lips brushed against hers.

"Ari… my friends call me Ari."

The lines around his eyes tightened as his irises flicked from her eyes to her mouth and back. "Am I your friend?"

"I'd like you to be," she tried to kiss him, but he held her at bay.

His left brow rose infinitesimally. "Maybe *more*?"

The cadence of his low, smooth voice sent a jolt of excitement to the pit of her belly, making her draw in a quivering breath, "Maybe…"

Without warning, his hands plunged into her hair, pulling her head closer, the forceful demand of his mouth overtaking her. When his tongue slipped past her lips, her eyes fluttered closed, and on a sigh she gave into the temptation that was Aaron McAvoy.

TINY TEMPTATIONS
A CUB FOR CHRISTMAS: CHAPTER FIVE

Sitting in the lobby of her hotel, Ari waited for Aaron's arrival. After their short lunch-time rendezvous and make-out session, he had dropped her off with the promise of giving her a night she'd never forget. Glancing at her watch, her tummy did a flip-flop when she realized that in ten short minutes, her cub would arrive.

Laughter suddenly barreled through her making several people seated near her give her sideways glances as if they were questioning her sanity. If Aaron was a *cub*, what did that make her? A stupid smile plastered itself on her face when she realized it made her a *cougar*. Not once in her life did she ever think that title would apply to her, even though her recently-engaged daughter, Violet, had called her as much. Actually, what Vi had called her was a MILF. She guessed her daughter had said that in hopes of bringing her spirits up after her college-sweetheart-turned-husband had left her for a younger version of herself. However, Ari had found the remark less than flattering. She didn't want to just be a mother that someone would like to fuck, she wanted a connection. Like the one she had found with Aaron. If she was going to have to wear a label, then *cougar* was most definitely one she could live with.

So there she sat, a forty-three-year-old *cougar,* waiting for her twenty-something-year-old *cub* to show up and hopefully sweep her off her feet for the weekend. And with any luck, make her forget just how long it had been since she had been fucked senseless. *One could hope, anyway.*

Five minutes earlier than his expected arrival time, Aaron walked through the doors of the hotel lobby, looking like an elegant, youthful Clark Gable circa early 1930's, right down to the faint dimple in his left cheek. Even his attire looked as if he had plucked it right from Gable's very own wardrobe. The dark-blue velvet blazer with a white silk pocket insert, blue and gray striped tie, and gray tweed pants that hung low on his hips and matching overcoat only accentuated his already charismatic good looks. But, his dark, nearly-black hair tousled to perfection and eyes as blue as the wintery night sky—were all his own.

Rising to greet him, she outstretched a hand to touch him to make sure he wasn't just a cruel, teasing dream. He wasn't, and when she placed her hand on his chest, the solid muscles beneath it sent a spike of heat rushing through her. Suddenly, going out felt like a pointless distraction. Before she could say as much, he reached into his pocket and pulled out two tickets.

"*A Boy from Oz*. Tonight's the last show for the one-week only revival. Original 2003 cast and all. I had a hell of time getting the tickets. How about it?"

When he put it like that, when he *said* it like that, with his sinfully rich, harmonious voice that made her toes curl—how could she deny him?

*

With the music from the play still tinkling inside her head, Ari found it nearly impossible to stop smiling. Aaron had a great sense of humor and she suspected he had chosen the musical for a specific reason. Or maybe not. She did have a tendency to

TINY TEMPTATIONS

read into things. However, when they drove away from the theatre to his company helipad and he began to hum a song from the show, *Only an Older Woman,* she was positive that he was trying to say something.

She got the message loud and clear. And she could play at his little innuendo game, too.

A quick search on her phone brought a well-known tune up. When *Simon and Garfunkle's* melodic voices chimed in to the tune of *Mrs. Robinson,* Aaron's eyes widened, a roguish smile graced his face and a howl of laughter filled the back seat, making his driver jump and glance over his shoulder.

"You have no idea how ironic it is that you just played that song," he continued to bubble over with amusement. She gave him a questioning look, but he shook his head. "I'll explain later."

Pulling her into his embrace, his mouth crashed down onto hers. He kissed her so thoroughly and possessively, for the few seconds that their intimate moment lasted, she felt as if she belonged to someone again.

"Thanks for the show," she whispered against his lips. "I loved it."

"The night's not over yet. Helicopter ride, then dinner. In that order, just in case you get a case of air sickness."

She grinned at him, "I've flown before, I'm sure I'll be fine."

"Flying in a helicopter is different. You'll see."

*

And it *was* different. Even as she sat there strapped into the small back compartment next to her Cub, her stomach did several somersaults before she settled into the uneasy feeling of flying a mere few thousand feet above the New York City skyline. Only when she was able to negotiate a truce with her stomach to accept the inevitability of the swoops and dips could she enjoy the view.

And what a view it was—a pale crescent moon slipping in and out of view behind a dark smudge of clouds against a black velvet sky… lightly blowing snow swirling across the frozen expanse below… brilliant lights in every color adorning buildings and windows.

With the helicopter smoothly hovering above the tall buildings, Aaron leaned into her, breaking her entrancement.

"Robinson," his husky voice barely resonated over the loud hum of the rotors.

"What?" she practically hollered so that she could be heard.

A naughty smirk curled his lips upward. "This helicopter is a Robinson R66 Turbine."

"No shit?"

"No shit!" he yelled over the loud wind whistling outside.

After pointing out the Empire State Building, the Metropolitan Museum of Art, the Rockefeller Center, and the building where his company headquarters was located, the pilot peered over his shoulder and yelled back, "The wind has really picked up. We need to bring her back in."

"I'm sorry, Ari," he gave her a look of disappointment when the helicopter turned back.

TINY TEMPTATIONS

"I'm not. This was incredible."

She reached a hand over to place on his thigh when a quick bump of turbulence made her palm graze his crotch. She hadn't meant to cop a feel; however, she had no regrets—most especially not when she felt the blood surge to his cock.

His eyes zoomed in on hers and one of his rare bashful smiles made an appearance as he chuckled at himself. "I'm sorry about that, too."

"Are you?"

His eyes narrowed with confusion. "Am I *what*?"

"Are you *really* sorry?"

He gave her an amused twitch of his mouth and pulled her close so he didn't have to shout anymore, "Only if you're offended."

"I'd be more offended if you hadn't shown a response."

"Well, then, I'm not sorry. And I'm more than happy to oblige."

Somehow, she didn't see Aaron as the type to *oblige* anyone. He was too confident, even if he did briefly show signs of nervousness. He seemed more like a take charge kind of man. *One could hope, anyway.*

Taking him by surprise, she glided her palm over the semi-rigid outline in his slacks. Back and forth, she rubbed—lightly at first, then with more pressure, gripping his cock as it continued to grow with each of her premeditated strokes.

"I guess you really are worth a *sizeable* amount."

His low seductive laugh barely masked a frustrated groan, and he grabbed her hand to guide it more purposefully along the head of his shaft. When he did, she tried to imagine what it looked like in the flesh. What it would *feel* like inside of her. Warm… thick… hard…. stretching her to full capacity…

She wanted him, and dinner, well, it could wait. She couldn't. She wasn't getting any younger, and like Aaron had so eloquently put it: *there was no time like the present.*

TINY TEMPTATIONS
A CUB FOR CHRISTMAS: CHAPTER SIX

"Can we forego dinner, at least for now?" Ari asked as the helicopter hovered and then landed.

Aaron's body stiffened and he pinned her with a look so fierce, she froze in her seat. Without answering, he swiftly unbuckled himself, and then her. Taking her by the hand, he helped her out and promptly tucked her into his body to protect her from the frigid gusts of air blasting against them.

Once inside his car, he turned to face her as he brought her wrist to his lips. "You said no to dinner, but I'm hungry, Ari. *So hungry.*"

The suggestiveness in his tone and statement left nothing to the imagination, and when his mouth brushed against the delicate skin of her inner wrist, she felt an overwhelming imperative to allow him to feast on her body.

"A growing boy needs to eat…"

Her statement was swiftly cut off by his hand in her hair and his tongue in her mouth. He broke from their kiss just long enough to bark an order to his driver, "My place," before ravaging her again.

She probably should've cared that another man was only a few feet away when Aaron's fingers slipped under her skirt and past her panties, but the fire he had kindled within her was burning too rapidly out of control. A bolt of lustful energy lanced through her at his neediness, and when his fingers found what they were seeking out and infiltrated her wet depths, a shiver of arousal shot through her at his dominant forcefulness.

Her fingers raked through his thick, soft hair when he took control of her and repositioned her body lengthwise on the seat. Maneuvering her, he hiked her skirt up without completely exposing her so that he had better access to what he wanted. As he pumped his digits in and out, her body flamed as the heat moved from the place he was concentrating his efforts on, up to her abdomen and breasts.

Everything that happened in the few minutes in the back of that Valiant seemed dreamlike and she suddenly felt like she was watching another Broadway play—one where the characters were all mouths, hands, body heat and desire as they melded into one another. It was a beautiful play, both erotic and sweet, and she was happy to be one of the lead characters for a change and not just some secondary one who only had a few lines of dialogue.

Was this really her life? Was this gentlemanly yet controlling and beautiful young man really hers for the evening? A nip to her collarbone stole what breath remained in her lungs and proved to her that, *yes,* this was her life and this man who seemed more like a naughty, courtly prince really was hers.

A short time later, they were in a parking garage and she was being dragged onto an elevator where Aaron's mouth was once again devouring her. Her insides swelled at the drugging scent of him as he slammed her against the wall, capturing her body with his. She took his hand and guided it up her skirt and past her panties again so that he could continue where he had left off, but the elevator ride stopped soon after it had begun.

Tripping over themselves, they entered his condo. In one swift motion, he swept her up into his arms and carried her the short distance to his bedroom and laid her out on his bed. As she lay there, watching him watch her, she allowed the slow throb pulsing through her body to consume her.

Perched on the edge of his bed, she tugged at the belt loops of his pants to draw him close and pressed a hand against the solid mass of masculinity pressed inside his pants.

She stood, her gaze climbing up his six foot frame to stare up into his eyes. "May I please unwrap my Christmas gift early?"

The light in his eyes grew wild, and a slow, cat-like grin spread across his face, revealing his well-hidden dimple. "You may."

Unhurriedly, she began unclothing him. First, she unbuckled his belt and pulled it through the loops with slow precision while she kept her eyes glued to his. Next, she removed his blazer, tugging it down off his shoulders as she pressed her breasts against him. The exquisite knot of desire in her belly tightened when he reached up to assist her by loosening his tie.

What wicked things would he do to her with that tie? Bind her wrists behind her? Or pin them high above her head like she had always wanted? *Maybe...*

When her eyes lingered a little too long on the tie in his hands, Aaron's finger on her chin drew her focus back to him.

"We can save that adventure for another day," he whispered as he tossed the tie onto his nightstand.

He had read her mind, though she doubted that would've been a difficult task at that point. She was an open book and she knew it.

"What happened to—*there's no time like the present*?" she teased.

He only smiled, but the gleam in his eyes let her know that he was taking notes. *One could hope, anyway.*

Picking up where she left off, she plucked each of his shirt buttons open, slowly revealing his smooth chest and dark hair below his naval that trailed down his abdomen.

When his pants and briefs were finally lying in a heap on the floor, she stepped back to take in the full vision of Aaron McAvoy. *He was absolutely beautiful*. Even in the darkness she could see what a spectacular specimen of man he was. And his cock—sweet heavens above. She had hit the holiday jackpot. It was long, thick and so unbelievably hard… she had never had so much to work with.

With the same leisurely pace she had unclothed him, he began to undress her. His fingertips grazed over her heated flesh, inch by sweet inch, and when he unsnapped her bra and tossed it aside, his hot, damp breath was felt on her neck. No movement on his part was wasted and it was absolute torture, but damn if it wasn't the sweetest kind.

She sat on the edge of the bed once more and pulled him toward her by his hips. With his shaft in her hands, she squeezed gently until a drop of pre-come appeared on the tip, and moaned at the taste of him as she took him into her mouth. She eased the pressure of her hold, stroking him carefully from base to tip. Her eyes flicked open and upward to watch the pleasure on his face as she swirled her tongue over the broad, hot head of his erection. His body began to sway and thrust into her grip, and when his breathing quickened and a guttural sigh vibrated in his throat, she freed him. Once his breathing slowed, she tormented him over and over, bringing him to the edge only to deny him. It was a cruel thing to do and frustration sparkled in his eyes, but the way his body responded to her, she couldn't deny herself the satisfaction. When she began to toy with him again, he gripped a handful of hair at the back of her head and leaned down as he got in her face.

"Lay back," he instructed.

Now it was his turn to tease her. And he did. Over and over, his tongue traced a path along her slit and dipped into her pussy alongside his fingers. Over and over, he pumped his fingers into her until she began to squirm uncontrollably. Over and over, he flicked his tongue against her clit and sucked at it as he brought her to the brink of climax, only to withdraw. He taunted and tantalized her with his mouth, tongue and fingers until she thought she'd lose her mind, and until her strained and excited voice became unfamiliar in her ears.

When he finally reached into a nightstand drawer to retrieve a condom, she nearly came undone. Just like watching a play, she loved this part: the anticipation and exhilaration of what was to come next.

With the foil wrapper tossed aside and his cock sheathed and ready to pleasure her, he positioned himself between her knees, the rough hair on his legs scraping the inside of her thighs as he nudged her legs wider. He rubbed the head of his cock over her clit and just when the musk and sweat of his body filled her nostrils, he lowered himself slowly so that she could accept the full thickness of him. She mewled as he pierced her to the hilt, his *sizeable* masculinity reaching places that had never been reached before.

Every roll of his hips seemed to be planned out as he watched her, gauging her response. With his body balanced over hers, she clawed her nails into his shoulders, arching eagerly up to meet his next thrust. When she wrapped her legs around his waist and dug her heels into the small of his back and lifted into him, she heard a ragged murmur of contentment in his throat. Assailed by sensation after sensation, small spasms of bliss began to pulse throughout her, and when her heart began to slam erratically against her rib cage, she tensed against him.

A quick flip later she was on her stomach and breathless as he began to pound into her once again. She clung to the bedding below her, her previously meticulously straightened dark-brown hair now lying in a wavy, sweaty mess all around her face. Harder, he pumped into her, reaching new depths.

But it wasn't just the depth that was driving her closer to the edge, it was his tempo. Just like when he had orally pleasured her, his slow rhythm of fucking her was bringing her closer to her finale. Like a well-tuned machine, he worked her body until a spasmodic tightening of her muscles signaled her impending release. When she briefly felt his teeth on her shoulder blade and then his mouth suddenly sucking ferociously against the tender flesh at the nape of her neck, she arched her back and pressed into the cock that was filling her, and cried out as her body trembled and an orgasm tore through her.

Only when her body stopped shuddering did he reposition their bodies so that she was sitting atop him. Taking the reins, she took his shaft into her fingers and guided it to her entrance. Slowly, she lowered herself onto him and rocked her body against his. The hot, heady scent of their mixed perfumes and sex filled her head, dizzying her with excitement.

Running his palms up her thighs, he gently parted her legs to get a better view, his eyes shimmering with pure arousal. His hands found her breasts and cupped them before moving up to frame her face in his large hands. Tugging her down against his chest, their lips pressed together in a sensual kiss. Without warning, his body tightened and his thrusts came faster. She braced herself against his chest and when he stilled and grunted, his gasp of release feathered along her senses like a warm summer breeze.

Gently disengaging from her, he removed the condom and curved his body protectively around her and burrowed his nose against her neck.

"That was fucking incredible," his smothered whisper was heard against her skin.

"Admit it," she pulled back to gaze into the bluest eyes she had ever seen, "this old lady totally rocked your world."

A deep, resounding laugh came from his full, sexy mouth before he responded, "I don't see any old lady here. I only see you."

The heat of embarrassment rose to her cheeks, though she didn't exactly know why. Maybe it was because his response was unsolicited. Or maybe it was because she suddenly felt like she had been fishing for a compliment. When she attempted to rise from his bed, he yanked her back down next to him.

"Stay the night. I've never woken up on Christmas Day wrapped up in a warm, naked, stunningly beautiful woman."

ELLA DOMINGUEZ

With a smile and a soft sigh, she curled on her side next to him and snuggled into his warmth. When he said it like that, how could she deny him?

TINY TEMPTATIONS
A CUB FOR CHRISTMAS: CHAPTER SEVEN

Waking up in the middle of the night to the smell of savory bacon along with sweet foods was a new experience for Aricelli. When she pried her eyes open, Aaron was seated on the edge of the bed with a breakfast tray in hand. She eyed the tray only to find it covered, veiling its contents.

"Merry Christmas, Beautiful," he smiled.

"To you as well. What time is it?" she glanced out the window to see it still dark outside.

"The time doesn't matter. It's officially Christmas," he stated resolutely as he reached for something on the night stand. "Hands in front of you," he quickly commanded.

Her eyes widened and thrill surged through her when she spied the tie she had been fantasizing about in his hands. Without hesitation, she crossed her wrists, one over the other, in front of her.

As he looped the silk fabric in and out of her wrists, his eyes shot to hers. "You're awfully trusting."

She narrowed her eyes at him and smiled evilly. "I can afford to be. I have a first degree black belt in Judo… working on my second."

A lazy taunting smile slid from one side of his finely stubbled jaw to the other, "That's so hot. And here I thought you were just this mild-mannered-mom-type from upstate who worked from home. What other sexy things do you do in your spare time?" his voice oozed curiosity.

"Hot yoga and Pilates."

"*Hot* indeed," he grinned. "No wonder you're so *bendy*. I need to seriously up my game if I'm going to keep up with you."

She laughed at his juvenile response, but felt a rush of heat rise to her cheeks from his flattering remark.

"You don't work out?" she huffed in disbelief.

"Not like *that.* Once, maybe twice a week I go to the gym for some cardio, but that's about it."

"Well, at your age, you can afford to be lazy," she watched as he knotted the tie. "That'll all change when you hit thirty. And forty? God, don't get me started. *Everything* about your body will change then."

A grin quirked his sensual lips, "You're so wise."

"Wiser than you."

"Maybe…"

"By the way, how old are you?" she finally asked.

"Nearly thirty."

"So, what… twenty-nine?"

"Nearly…" he avoided her gaze.

When she swallowed loudly from nervousness, Aaron's eyes darted to hers. "Lighten up. What we have going on between us is a great thing."

"How old, Aaron?" she persisted.

He sighed and rolled his eyes. "Twenty-eight… and three-quarters if you want to get technical."

"God," she slumped into the bed. "You're only five years older than my daughter."

"Ha!" his voice barreled through him. "That's pretty sweet, don't you think? You and me? A beautiful, smart, fit older woman and a sexy-as-fuck young entrepreneur getting it on? Come on, this is fantastic. Not even in my wildest, wettest teenage dreams did I ever think I'd get this lucky. Don't be so uptight. Older men date younger women everyday of the week and no one thinks twice about it. What's the difference here? You gravitate to whomever the hell you gravitate towards. Age, sex, race, religion... none of that matters so long as there's a connection, and that's what we have. I felt it the first time you checked me out."

Awestruck, Ari could only stare back at him. She wasn't being uptight, just cautious. But he was right. Hell, her husband had left her for a younger woman and no one gave two shits about it. Although Aaron was showing his immaturity, she couldn't stop herself from laughing at him. He was adorable. And, in his own way, wise. And, yes, he *was* sexy-as-fuck.

"Wow. You are full of yourself, aren't you?" she was finally able to get out between laughs.

"I have every right to be. A cougar totally *rocked my world* last night," he mocked her.

"True, but for future reference, you were the one who checked me out," she kiddingly defended herself.

"That's not how I remember it. As far as I'm concerned, it was a mutual checking out. Now, hush. I have plans for you."

From out of nowhere, a charcoal-gray angora scarf appeared in his hands. Swiftly, he wrapped it around her eyes, shielding everything from her view and blocking the light. After a few manipulations, he seemed satisfied with its placement.

"Open that perfect mouth of yours, Beautiful," he whispered.

When she complied, she felt something moist touch her lips. Next, the sweet smell of watermelon filled her nostrils along with bacon.

"Have you ever tried these two combinations together?" he asked as he placed them into her mouth.

She shook her head. She hadn't. And there she was again, experiencing something new with this younger man—this man who probably hadn't even experienced true love yet. Or maybe he had. She had no idea.

As she chewed on the oddly delicious combination of food that he had presented her, she let the flavors saturate her palate and tried to envision what his wild-blue eyes looked like as they watched her.

Bite after bite was pressed to her lips for her to sample, each nibble occasionally interspersed with a sensual kiss and sip of water 'to clear her palate.' He then explained as to why he thought each combination went well together, and further enlightened her as to his reasoning behind blindfolding and binding her. It was so that she could taste the food without distraction and enjoy each flavor profile, he said. And he was right—it had worked. Being only allowed a few of her senses while being fed from Aaron's hand proved to be the most eye-opening and sensual thing she had ever experienced.

She basked in the moment while wondering what it was about this man that was so intriguing. A man, for all intents and purposes, she didn't know anything about except that he was a successful business owner who had a taste for vintage cars, and a seemingly rocky relationship with his parents.

Suddenly, she remembered his statement about his mother being a dancer and not really seeing what was in front of her and about his family avoiding each other on the holidays. Is that was she was to him? *A mother-figure*? Like a woman who dates an older man looking for her father-figure? All at once, she wasn't turned on anymore. She didn't want to be anyone's mother-figure except to her children. *Why the hell did she have to always over think things?*

"Can you untie me, please?" she asked when she suddenly lost her appetite.

"Sure," Aaron answered without hesitation.

When he removed the scarf and her eyes met his, she felt disheartened. She had enjoyed her time with him, but it was time to leave.

Excusing herself to the bathroom, she quietly dressed and tried to slip out his front door before he could stop her. Just as she cracked the door open, she felt Aaron's hands on her shoulders.

"Were you really going to try to sneak out of here without saying goodbye?" Hurt tinged his words.

"Life is a like a play, Aaron," she heard herself saying. "It's full of characters: main characters, secondary characters, even background characters," she couldn't bring herself to face him and those amazing eyes. "Not all of them make it to the second act. Some of them are simply there to enhance the atmosphere," she swallowed noisily. "That's all I am: a background character—someone who, I hope, has enhanced your life in some tiny way, but not someone who was meant to be a main character."

"What happened? You were fine just a moment ago," she heard over her shoulder. She was quickly spun around and forced to face him. "And are you seriously comparing us to a play?"

"I had an amazing time with you, but it's time for me to exit-left," she reached behind her and gripped the door knob.

"Where is this coming from?"

She didn't dare speak of her fears that had unexpectedly reared their ugly heads. Not just the one about her being a mother-figure to him, but the fear that he would eventually want someone younger later down the road. Or, maybe someone who could give him a child. Or, perhaps someone who could keep up with him as she got older. All of them absurd, sure, especially considering this was most likely just a weekend fling. No matter, those nasty fears were there and she'd rather save face now than prolong things only to end up with a broken heart, or worse, break his still-optimistic-heart.

"It's Christmas, Ari" he whispered sadly as he reached up to drag a thumb across her lower lip.

"Let's not ruin the fantasy," she turned away and opened the door.

Gently, he pushed it closed. "Fuck the fantasy. I just want one more *real* night with you."

A lump clogged in her throat at his agonized whisper. *Yes, one more night*. Like Aaron had pointed out, it was Christmas, and how could she deny him on a day that was meant to be spent in celebration? Especially when he wouldn't be spending it with his family?

Pushing her fears aside, she smiled up at him and rose on her tiptoes to meet his lips. "Okay. One more night."

TINY TEMPTATIONS
A CUB FOR CHRISTMAS: CHAPTER EIGHT

This thing with Aaron would be nothing more than what it was meant to be: a two-night-stand. Aricelli promised herself that when he took her hand into his and walked her toward the expansive window in his living room to gaze out.

Glancing to her left, a photo sitting on the mantle of his electric fireplace caught her attention. In the photograph was a ballerina decked out in full tutu holding a bouquet of roses and standing next to a small boy. Releasing her hand from Aaron's, she approached the mantle to get a better look, dreading what she might see. If she looked anything like the woman in the photo, she would most likely wretch and then run screaming from his apartment.

To her absolute relief, there were no similarities between herself and the dancer in the ornately framed picture. In fact, they looked nothing alike. His mother, blonde and blue-eyed, stood at least five inches taller than herself. Actually, Aaron didn't even look like her. She scrutinized the image, trying to see the familial resemblance, but could find none other than the eye color. Then again, the image was slightly discolored from age. She stared at the snapshot one last time before shifting her gaze back onto Aaron, and then back to the photo, still finding it hard to believe that the same woman in the photo could've given birth to him.

As if sensing her disbelief, he responded, "I get my looks from my father's side of the family. Also," he tucked her hair behind her ear, "my hair was much lighter when I was younger."

"Younger than what?" she giggled.

"Real cute," he wrapped an arm around her shoulders.

Staring at the image a moment longer, her own children popped into her head. Their smiles, their laughter, the love she felt for them… Here it was, Christmas, and she couldn't even enjoy the day with them.

"I need to call my kids," she looked up at Aaron.

"Absolutely. I'm sure they're dying to hear from their mother."

"And you," she ran her fingers through his hair, "call your mother. I'm sure she's dying to hear from her son."

"I doubt it," he mumbled and walked back toward the window.

"Humor me, Aaron." Unmoving, he stared out at the fresh snow that was still coming down. "Come on, it's Christmas. Don't be a Grinch."

Turning his head to the side, he peered over his shoulder at her with one eyebrow raised. "Bah hum bug."

"That's Scrooge, not the Grinch."

"Oh, that's right; you know your *plays* don't you?"

Ugh. He had just called her out on her little monologue and now, having seen the photo of his mother, her overdramatic reaction felt slightly ridiculous. Ignoring the sting of his comeback, she found her clutch and phone, and dialed Vi's number knowing that both she and her son, Vance, would be together.

When her daughter answered, a combination of joy and sadness filled her heart. Put on speaker phone, she was able to have a brief conversation with both of her kids, making their absence somewhat acceptable.

"We miss you, Mom," Violet's tear-smothered voice rang out.

"Please, don't do that," she begged.

This was the first Christmas she had ever spent way from her kids and she choked back a sob at the pain in Vi's voice. Their bond went beyond a typical mother-daughter relationship. Or maybe it didn't. She didn't really know anyone else with whom she could compare their relationship to. But for her—Vi was her best friend, her BFF, her mini-me.

When the news came out that Vi's father had been having an affair with a younger woman and was leaving her mother to take up with said floozy, Vi had staunchly defended her mother and cut off all contact with her father. It was sweet, but heartbreaking. Especially considering that Vi had been very close with her father as well. Putting their differences aside for the sake of her children, Ari had insisted that Vi forgive her father and try to mend their relationship, regardless of whether or not she could do the same. She hoped Vi and her fiancé were behaving themselves while at her father's and at least treating his new wife with a tiny bit of respect, even if that home wrecker didn't deserve it.

As for her son, well, he had tried to remain indifferent and unbiased during the whole ordeal. It was an admirable trait that would serve him well when he became a lawyer. Now a junior in college, he was too busy with his own life to pay much attention to the goings on of his now-divorced-parents. And Ari didn't blame him nor did she mind. The fact was that she was glad he had something to preoccupy himself with.

"Look, Vi, I'm not at home and I don't want to get all sappy here," she tried to end their phone call before she completely broke down.

"Where are you?"

"In the city. I came here to take my mind off of things for a few days."

Just then, Aaron called out to her causing Vi to perk up.

"Oh my God, is that a man's voice? Where *exactly* are you?"

Now she wished she hadn't mentioned not being at home because she hated lying to her daughter. Anyway, she was terrible at it.

"At…," she tried to think of a suitable white-lie but could think of none. "A friend's house."

"Friend, as in a friend-with-benefits?"

God, Vi could be blunt. And nosy. Yet more of her own traits that had rubbed off on her daughter. Yes, Vi truly was a mini version of herself.

"Yes, Violet Anne, there are benefits involved," she bluntly answered back.

"Is he cute?" she brimmed with interest.

"Oh yes, definitely cute," she answered without revealing anything more.

"Is he…"

"Enough. I have to go. Tell your brother I love him and miss you both."

"Fine, but be prepared to face the Violet Inquisition when I see you again. Do you have a message for Dad?" her sarcastic irony was ill-concealed.

TINY TEMPTATIONS

She laughed at her daughter's obstinacy. That she definitely got from her father. "Not a message per se, just a reminder that there's no return on the cunt-seeking missile I've sent to him and his new wife for Christmas."

Vi's laughter boomed in her ear. "Be careful and I love you. And on second thought, just to be safe, text me the name of your *cute* lover."

"Yes, *Mom*," Ari joked. "I love you, too, My Girl. Bye."

After ending her phone call and doing as her daughter had requested, she found Aaron in the living room cueing up music on his stereo. When he turned to face her, his wide grin greeted her.

"Cunt-seeking missile, huh? That's pretty harsh," he chuckled. "I hope I'm never the recipient of one of those."

"You heard that?" her face flushed with embarrassment. "What else did you hear?"

In two long strides he cut the distance between them and gave her a roll of his shoulders. "Nothing important," he gripped her waist and hauled her into his arms.

As they began to dance around the room to the unfamiliar song, the lyrics suddenly struck a chord—*Friends with Benefits.*

"Nothing important," he repeated, "that is, unless *benefits* are important to you," he dipped her and smiled down at her. "They're important to me… being a *friend* and all."

So, he had heard that, too. This man—he definitely had a sense of humor. And boy did he love ribbing her.

Kicking her shoes off, she danced the remainder of the song in his arms, tightly clutching his well-toned body and enjoying the way he moved. She was glad she had stayed, even if it was for only one more night. Another dip and a twirl later and the song ended.

But Ari wanted more and she could give just as good as she could get. Gliding to his stereo, she synced her phone to it and cued her own song of choice.

My Young Man promptly began to tinkle through the speakers when Aaron slid up behind her. In a heartbeat, she felt his hot, greedy hands roaming endlessly over her body.

"So you think I'm *cute,* huh?" he nipped at her earlobe.

"Definitely," she tipped her head to the side to give him access to the soft flesh of her neck.

Accepting her invitation, his lips trailed a sensuous path to her collar bone. "Maybe more than just cute?" his slid the strap of her dress off her shoulder to ghost his lips over her shoulder blade.

When his fingers deftly began to undress her at his usual slow pace, a throb sprang up between her legs. "Maybe…"she murmured.

"Technically, cute means attractive in a childlike way," he growled as he spun her around and glared down at her. "I'm no child, Ari. I'm a grown man with needs and desires that I can't even begin to put into words."

When she came face to face with him, his playful look had disappeared and only primal sexual hunger stared back at her. In that moment, she couldn't recall ever feeling so tight with need.

TINY TEMPTATIONS

"Technically, it also means sharply intelligent, young and physically attractive," she countered with bated breath when his arms crushed her in his embrace.

"Is that how you see me?" his eyes narrowed.

"Yes," she whispered as he squeezed the last bit of breath from her lungs and plunged a hand into her hair.

He drew her head back to meet his heated gaze. "Good, because I don't want to be cute or adorable to you, Ari. I want to be strong in your eyes. I want to be superhuman." He grazed his jaw against her ear and growled low in his throat, "I want to be the man you can't get enough of."

Damn it. *That voice*. If that growled whisper was the last thing she heard before taking her last dying breath, she would have passed over to the other side a happy woman.

And those eyes? She felt as if she had been slammed in the chest at the galvanizing look he was giving her. My, God... *how could she deny him*?

A CUB FOR CHRISTMAS: CHAPTER NINE

Sweaty and breathless, Ari basked in the afterglow of yet another amazing encounter with Aaron. Her body ached in places and ways that it hadn't for years after proving to him just how *bendy* she really was.

Lying on her back and staring up at the ceiling, she wondered why she had waited so long to allow herself the pleasure of being with another man after her husband. It had been nearly a year and a half since her divorce was finalized, and longer than that since the last time she had sex. Well, with someone other than herself, that is.

Rolling onto her side, she watched as Aaron lay with his eyes closed, catching his breath. Reaching a hand up, she rubbed the scruff on his face. His five o'clock shadow was more like baby-beard now and it was quite a look for him. Clean-shaven, he looked much younger, but like this, naked and furry, he looked damned handsome.

His eyes popped open and he rolled onto his side, tucking his arm under his head and pushing her sweat-dampened locks away from her face. In an instant, he disappeared into the next room. She could hear his voice, low and throaty, speaking in whispered tones. It was only a few minutes later that he reappeared, looking disappointed.

"My Mom," he answered her unspoken question.

"Thank you for calling her."

"I didn't do it for you."

She drew close to him when he laid back down next to her. "I know you didn't, but thank you anyway." His look of sadness waned and his previous look of serenity rematerialized. "Do you have any siblings?" she questioned him, curious about his life outside the four walls they were sharing for the night.

"No. One mistake was enough for my mom."

"Oh, Aaron," Ari suddenly felt like crying, "don't say that. You were *not* a mistake. You were a surprise."

Disbelief flashed in his eyes, "What's the difference?"

Propped up on an elbow, she grazed her nails over his scalp and through his hair as she explained exactly what the difference was. "A surprise is something you don't know you want until you get it."

His eyes roamed over her face as if not comprehending why she was so upset. "I suppose, but it's true about my being a mistake. I wasn't planned and my arrival derailed my mom's dancing career. She's never forgiven me for that," he leaned back to stare up at the ceiling again. "Or my father. She's always held a bit of resentment towards him, too."

"Do you have a good relationship with him?"

"It's okay. We talk and do things together on occasion. I guess you could say we've bonded over my mother's disliking of us. It's hard for him always trying to keep the peace, you know? Poor guy, he's a romantic-at-heart and just wants to please my mother."

"A romantic-at-heart. So, you do take after him."

One side of Aaron's mouth lifted and he quickly glanced at her. "Yeah, I suppose I do take after him in that regard, too. It's too bad being romantic doesn't get you anywhere in this city."

Her insides twisted at the gloominess reflected back in his eyes. "You've had your heart broken?"

His brows slanted downward into a frown. "Too many times to count."

He was being so forthcoming, she couldn't resist asking more. "Have you ever been married?"

"Once. Briefly." Understanding suddenly shined in his irises. "A surprise. Yeah. I get it. Like my son. He wasn't planned either, but he was the best damn thing to ever happen to me."

Ari's heart swelled. "You have a son?"

He nodded. "I share custody with his mom. I wish I could spend more time with him and it sucks that I can't spend Christmas with him, but I'll call him first thing in the morning. Things may have not worked out between us, but, fortunately, she's a great with him. I'm lucky for that." His gaze drifted for a split second as if conjuring up his son's image in his mind. "He's such a great kid," he beamed with pride and then laughed. "A tenacious little-fucker and so damned funny."

"Like his father," she kidded, tugging at his earlobe. "What's his name?"

"Jacob. *Jake*. My mini-me."

She sat up and practically shouted, "That's what I call my daughter!"

Reaching for his phone on the night stand, he brought up a song, *You Sexy Thing,* before turning back onto his side to face her again.

"You and your songs. You're not even subtle about the subliminal messages that you're trying to send," she huffed with a shake of her head.

"There's no need to be subtle when you're a sexy motherfucker." He smiled and snickered. "*Motherfucker*," he repeated with sarcastic emphasis as he snorted at his own joke. "Get it? I'm a…"

TINY TEMPTATIONS

"I get it," she said with a roll of her eyes. As her gaze became fixed on him, she felt embarrassed for having made all the wrong assumptions about him. "You know, you've surprised me. You're not at all the man I thought you were."

His brows shot up. "Surprised in a good way?"

"Definitely good."

He grinned, a quick flash of undiluted charm before tugging the comforter up over her exposed body and snuggling into her.

A few minutes passed when another song began to play, *December,* by yet another band she would've figured someone Aaron's age would never have heard of. Again, she had figured him all wrong.

Scooting up in the bed and resting his back against the headboard, he gazed down at her.

"So, look, I know I said only one more night, but…," he touched her chin, "there's a company New Year's Eve party and…" He sighed and chewed the corner of his lip. "I'd love for you to go with me."

Faced with his proposition, sadness settled in her gut again. "You know, Aaron, in a perfect world this thing between us would work out. But the world isn't perfect…"

Promptly, he cut in. "Please don't get all philosophical on me again. I don't think I can take another one of your speeches," he grumbled as he shook his head, making her smile. "I know this world isn't perfect. Believe me, *I know.* And I admit that I have a tendency to romanticize things, but I'm positive that I'm not making things up in my head when I say that we have a genuine connection," he pleaded his case.

"It's only been a few days…" she continued in an attempt to make him see her point, but he swiftly put his hand over her mouth.

"Hear me out. A day, a week, a month—it makes no damned difference. This thing between us—it's real, Ari. I'm not asking for a lifetime commitment from you…" A coy smile briefly flashed across his face. "*Yet*. I'm just asking for another date. Or two. Or ten. Or, however many it takes for us to get to know each other and decide if this thing will work out or not. That's all. Maybe it'll work out and maybe it won't. I mean, hell, maybe you'll realize that I grind my teeth at night, or that I leave wet towels on the bathroom floor, and decide that those are deal breakers. But, we owe it to ourselves to see where this thing will go."

His words were hitting all the right marks and his argument was valid, but still… "We live in different cities."

"Well, then, it's a good thing I own a helicopter, isn't it?" He quickly shut her down. When she sat silently trying to come back with another rebuttal, he huffed, "Give it up, woman. Just say yes."

Again, she sat speechless and mortified at the thought of pursuing a relationship with him.

Persistent as ever, Aaron gripped her shoulders before he presented his final appeal.

"Let me put it to you in terms that you can understand. Life is like a play, and sometimes that play ends. But sometimes, *sometimes,* it comes back stronger and with a better cast. It's revived. There are continuations and sequels and spin-offs, and the characters who were only background characters in the original show suddenly take the center stage. But the thing is—you're not a background character, Ari.

TINY TEMPTATIONS

You're a leading lady, and this production doesn't have to end. It can just keep going on and on, even if the action isn't happening on the stage, because sometimes all the good stuff is happening back stage. The show is what you make of it. Anyway," his voice trailed off, his dark lashes half lowering over his eyes in a sensual gaze, "any form of reality with you is far better than any one of my fantasies could ever be."

Before she could respond, he laid a kiss on her lips that was so fierce and hot, it stifled any objections that were still lingering within her.

"Do you understand?" he asked when his lips released hers.

Hell yes, she understood. How could she not when he put it like that, when he *kissed* her like that. And with those eyes the color of nightshade staring back at her with pure longing—*how could she deny him*?

She couldn't and so, she didn't, because as it turned out, Aaron *was* the man she couldn't get enough of.

The End
Or is it just the beginning?

Like these characters? Want more of their story?
Message Ella and let her know.

ELLA DOMINGUEZ

THE 12 KINKS OF CHRISTMAS

Copyright © Ella Dominguez, 2014
All Rights Reserved

TINY TEMPTATIONS

THE 12 KINKS OF CHRISTMAS: ACKNOWLEDGEMENTS

Thank you to my loyal fans and AMAZING beta readers. Without them, I would be alone and discouraged with my grammatically incorrect writings.

Thank you to Eva Simone for asking me to participate in this anthology. Also, for putting this wonderful group of authors together! Her hard work is greatly appreciated, especially during the busy holiday season.

ELLA DOMINGUEZ

THE 12 KINKS OF CHRISTMAS: CREATIVE

On the first day of December, my Lover gave to me - a delicious flogging while bound to an old oak tree.

My lover is the Dominant to my submissive, you see. He is the Ruler of My Universe. My Master. He says *jump* and I say, *Yes, Sir.* It's the wickedest of trade-offs - his gift of authority for my obedience. The exchange hardly seems fair for all that I receive in return, yet he reassures me that what I am giving him is just as rewarding.

It's not a lifestyle for everyone, but it's the way of life I've chosen. To live any other way would be unfulfilling.

My Sir does not believe in the *Christ* in Christmas, as I do, but we compromise as we do in all areas of our life. He is an agnostic, sensual sadist, and me, a born and raised Christian who enjoys anal sex. Don't judge. It works.

I prefer to think of my One and Only as *flognostic* as he has a particular talent for wielding said sexual apparatus. It's his favorite tool of the trade and the reason he has chosen it to kick off the holiday season. This is our first Christmas together. While he's been meticulously planning everything out, I've been anxiously awaiting his 12 Kinks of Christmas. He has plotted out the course for my pleasure, because he's creative like that.

And so the 12 Kinks have begun.

I'm led outside clad in only winter boots, lingerie, and a blindfold. With the frigid air nipping at my nips, my chilled body heats from the inside out.

TINY TEMPTATIONS

Wrapping soft nylon rope around my wrists and ankles, he binds me to the oak tree that he planted with his parents as a child. The sound of his breathing reveals his excitement, yet his movements remain unhurried. His hands, determined to have their way with me, show the skill held within them.

I am stripped of my vision, magnifying the sounds, sensations and smells all around me.

A gust of glacial air bites into my flesh, sending a shiver of goose bumps over every inch of my body. The scent of our fireplace… His cologne – fresh cut grass, citrus, and lavender… The searing heat of the leather against my skin… Each moment, *exquisite*.

The flames of desire licking up my spine… The buzz in my brain and limbs from his manipulations… All of it, *divine.*

The caress of his fingers on my cheeks and the adoration felt in his touch when I beg for more… Every bit of it, *essential.*

The cowhide against my belly, red welts, and pain - I'm riding the fine edge between *not enough* and *almost too much*. His unrelenting rhythm is slow and deliberate, yet never unkind. His attention, unwavering and focused, and there's never a subtle movement of my body missed.

His voice, thick and steady, is dripping with power when he asks, "Will you fly for me today, Butterfly?"

But it's not a question; it's a command. *Yes, I will fly for you today, Sir.* The statement hovers on my lips, but I am unable to form the words.

The chill has left my body as warmth encircles me like a heated blanket thrown around my torso and shoulders. The tingling in my toes has worked its ways upward to my thighs and pussy where the dull aching throb lingers. As his fingers slip into the deepest part of me, wet and slick with my arousal, sensation settles low in my belly and finally, creeps up to my brain.

My wings have spread. I'm so close to taking flight I can feel the wind under me, lifting me and taking a hold of me.

He presses the length of his body against me giving me his heat while his mouth takes possession of mine, his tongue dancing and swirling in time with the beat of my heart. His long, powerful fingers pump into me while a thumb circles around my clit, setting my nerves and senses on fire.

The zip of his pants... The head of his cock near my entrance... His thickness pushed into me...Warm, rigid, full of urgency.

I have pleased him; I can feel it in the throbbing of his shaft. I belong to him; I can hear it whispered on his lips.

And it happens. The thing that keeps me chained willingly to this man: he makes me fly, handing me over to the clouds and setting me free as he plunges into me over and over. The warmth in my belly cascades downward until my body convulses, and his name slips past my lips.

The rasp of his beard on my cheek, his damp breath near my ear, and a deep rumble emits from this throat, "Happy holidays, Butterfly."

It's a holiday memory that will forever be etched into my mind.

Eleven more kinks to go...

TINY TEMPTATIONS

THE 12 KINKS OF CHRISTMAS: FESTIVE & ORNERY

On the fifth day of December, my Lover gave to me, a wireless vibrating egg and a dildo shaped like a mini Christmas tree.

This week I get two kinks for the price of one, because he's festive like that.

My Dominant is nefarious in his ways. He dresses me to the nines in a red, velvet mini-dress and heels that will make my feet ache for days. He applies my make-up sparingly and touches up my lipstick, caring for me in the way only he can.

Kneeling before me, he slides my thigh-high stockings up my legs sensually, reminding with his touch that no other man will ever satisfy me.

Then, the fun begins. He eases the egg into my depths. As he gazes up at me with his sparkling hazel eyes, his mouth ravages my pussy while he cups my hips and pulls me close.

"Absolutely stunning..." He breathes against my mound.

The heat of an orgasm builds, but I'm denied, because he's ornery like that.

A company business party is on the agenda. A night filled with boring conversations and awkward silences; a night when many will drink too much and act foolishly. Yet, here we are, amongst a large group, sitting alongside his colleagues while an egg rests within the deepest recesses of my cunt.

The taste of warm cinnamon and apple cider is on my lips. The smell of pine and peppermint from the oversized Christmas tree and ornate candy canes tickles my nose. It's a joyous occasion and one that should be cherished, even if I'm not keen on large groups.

When a low vibration jolts my system, the blaze of desire fills my Dominant's eyes as they transfix on my expression. My eyes dart around, the heat of embarrassment rising to my cheeks, but no one notices.

He smiles and moistens his lips in that enticing way that reminds me where his tongue has been and where it *will* be. The slightest quirk of his eyebrow reveals his plans to deliver more. Voices around us drone on, and suddenly, more vibration. My eyes widen as does his boyish grin. Ornery doesn't come anywhere close to an accurate description for my Lover. He's determined, on a mission, and unrelenting in his naughty ways.

The pulse and buzz within me intensifies and my breath hitches. The slow roll in my stomach, the tripping of my pulse... Will this never end?

"Have you been to the new museum?"

A woman's voice breaks through my aroused state. I can't speak, if I do, I fear everyone will hear the excitement within my response, so I simply nod.

The sexual tension between me and my Lover is a constant undercurrent and though we may be in a crowded room, I've never felt closer to him. He watches me, and I wait for more pleasure in the solitude of our sensuality.

He rises and moves to the other side of the room. The vibration ceases, giving me a chance to catch my breath, but the moment is short-lived. The rhythmic throb within me causes me to press my thighs together to satiate the need for release building within me.

TINY TEMPTATIONS

I give him a look of distress. I can't come here. Not *here.* His eyes light up knowingly. I bolt upright and make a mad dash to the ladies room when he reaches out, his long fingers wrapping around my wrist and halting my escape.

"Please, Sir…" I plead with him.

"That's it, beg…"

He loves the begging. And I love giving him what he wants. Wrapping my arms around his waist, I press my breasts against him. "Please, My Lover, may I come?"

Someone nearby to us glances in our direction with a look of shock, but I don't care if they hear me, and neither does my Sir.

"Yes, Butterfly, come for me."

He reaches into his pocket, retrieving something. He places the Christmas tree into my hand and nods toward the lavatory.

"You won't join me?" I pout.

"Not this time," he winks. "Replace the egg when you're finished."

I excuse myself to find the largest stall available. Propped up in the toilet with my dress hiked over my hips, I remove the egg by pulling on the string and place into my handbag. I'm wet with excitement, and the tree slides into me with ease. In and out, I push it in deep, then shallow, tipping it upward to hit my G-spot. Over and over I repeat the motion until my pussy shoots off in waves all around it. I muffle my scream against the back of my hand when a group of women enter the room. A few giggles are heard as I bask in the aftermath of my release.

Four minutes flat is all the time it took to reach orgasm. Oh, that lovely egg…

With shaky legs, I rinse the egg and replace it. Upon exiting the restroom, my Lover is propped up against the wall just outside, waiting for me with a look of pure lust on his face.

He reaches for me, his rare sexual aura radiating off him like the heat of a blue-hot flame. "Did you save some for later?"

"Oh, yes. There's plenty left."

His seductive whisper and words stroke over me with the effect of a powerful kiss, "Good girl."

Nine more kinks to go…

TINY TEMPTATIONS

THE 12 KINKS OF CHRISTMAS: MYSTERIOUS & GENEROUS

On the eleventh day of December, my Lover gave to me – the promise of a kinky fantasy.

When I asked for a hint before leaving for work, he laughed softly, "We three Kings."

He said nothing more, because he's mysterious like that.

Snow on the ground makes for a long drive home. My anticipation is gnawing at me when I arrive to our humble abode from a long day at work, and I'm momentarily disappointed to see he has guests joining us for dinner. However, I freshen up and present myself to him with a smile on my face. It's the least I can do for this man who satisfies me unconditionally.

We three Kings.

The words hover in my mind like the memory of a delicious dream that still has me aroused even after awakening. He's not a God-fearing man nor does he believe in a higher deity, yet he has used the biblical term as a form of compromise. Or perhaps it was simply meant as a pun. It was probably the latter, being as his sense of humor is always on point.

I should know by now that my Sir is quite literal. When he said the next kink on the schedule was *We Three Kings*, he meant it. Literally. Tonight he is giving me two more gifts rolled into one mouth-watering package. As the three-well built men sit around the dining room table, my gaze drifts over them, my body heating with each lingering visual caress they give me.

They want me. And my Master will share, because he's generous like that.

"Come to me, Butterfly," my King gestures to his lap.

I comply, snuggling into his embrace. Clamping my face with his big hands, he shamelessly captures my mouth and delivers a full contact, wet-tongued, tonsil-probing kiss. Subtly, he shifts so the hot, hard outline of his erection cradles snugly between my thighs. My hands reach up and systematically remove his tie. I've done it a million times it seems and I no longer need my sight to perform this task.

Without opening my eyes, the sound of the table being cleared off makes me impatient to be drowning in men; in their tastes and scents, and the feeling of their erotically sinful movements as they take me, make me, and fuck me into the next holiday season.

Foreign, gentle hands tip my head back away from my Sir. Hunter-green eyes are watching me, silently demanding my attention. My Lover's fingers pluck at the buttons of my blouse as King Number Two brushes his firm, full, sexy lips back and forth over mine.

I'm lifted onto the table and my clothing removed as a low growl of approval vibrates through me. *I want this.* I've wanted it since I can remember. I had never spoken out loud of this fantasy until I met my One and Only. *My Sir.* All of my fantasies have since been shared with him. There are no secrets between us and for the gift of my honesty, I'm being rewarded with this thing that I've craved.

As the second and third Kings take control of my body, my Sir stands watching, unafraid and man enough to share me because he knows that there is no other man for me. He knows without a doubt, that he is the *only* King that matters.

TINY TEMPTATIONS

All of my senses are being tantalized... *Luscious lips wandering over me, sucking, licking and teasing... The mingled scents of aftershave and masculinity... Mouths wandering across my cheekbones, eyelids and chin. My Lover nuzzling my ear and nipping at my neck.*

"Such a beautiful, obedient Butterfly. Wouldn't you agree, Gentleman?"

"Yes," they answer in unison.

My King's words and deep wet kisses... The taste of other men... What have I done to deserve such ecstasy? Someone tell me so that I may do it again and again and again...

With my legs spread apart, I rock my hips against the mouth and tongue stroking in and out of me.

Another softly spoken command from my King. "That's it, fuck his mouth..."

My body is dragged to the end of the table and my head dipped off the edge for my throat to be penetrated.

"Bury yourself inside her throat as deeply as you can, and don't finish until you've gotten your fill," my Lover orders King Number Three.

Words are spoken between them, offering them guidance and leadership. My Lover knows my limits and shares them, pointing them in the direction of how to properly please me.

I force my eyes open and glance around the room. They have all stripped off their clothing and the bright overhead light bathes their bodies in illumination, highlighting their hard lines and the V of their pelvic muscles. The men's bodies around me are all hot, hard and as ready as I am. *Such a beautiful sight...*

My body arches with the need for release when my throat is delved into. I concentrate and will myself to open up for him. Wet and deep, he pushes into me and I hold my breath. I can do this… I've done it a million times it seems…

King Number Two climbs on top of the table in anticipation of claiming his prize, and straddles me with my legs between his.

Pressure against my pussy. The thick ridge of a condom covered cock breaching my entrance. The familiar stroking of my Sir's fingers felt against my clit, moving in time with King Number Two's thrusts.

My vision blurs from the deep and relentless push past my tonsils.

I don't want this to end…

Our bodies move in creative combination as my Lover manipulates my body so that he can take what belongs only to him – my ass. He moves behind King Two and directs him to push my knees up to my chest, tilting my hips upward. I am exposed completely, and helpless to resist the sensations being thrust upon me - unadulterated, male savagery and wanton desires.

And then, my favorite part. My Sir's tongue darts into me, licking up my ass crack lubricating me with his saliva. Fingers poked into my rectum – one, then two, easing in and out, stretching me and preparing me. Patiently he works another finger into me all the while I'm becoming breathless from my oral assault.

My Sir groans roughly as he slides himself into me. Balls deep, my ass clenches around him and grips him.

More sensations than my brain can comprehend… *Double penetrated. Triple penetrated.*

TINY TEMPTATIONS

Our bodies moving back and forth. Cocks sliding in and out of me; deep and shallow, rough and gentle.

The smell of men and sex is all around me. Raspy breaths and strained groans fill the room. We're all close, our bodies tightening with need. I'm dripping with arousal, and their bodies are covered in a sheen of sweat as we all fuck in unison toward one common goal.

King Three is the first to let go, his warm, salty release splashing against the roof of my mouth. One last plunge into my throat and he staggers backward to a chair as I swallow his Christmas gift.

King Two is the next to climax, my body milking him of his orgasm as small tremors run through him.

The last man standing is my King, but he paces himself and readjusts our bodies into a more comfortable position as he leans down onto me. His sharp teeth graze my shoulder as he thrusts into me. A tip of his pelvis and he makes me squeal like a schoolgirl. His fingers inserted into me caress my G-spot, making me whimper and writhe beneath him. Over and over, he hits it while pounding and slamming into me... Mercilessly... Adoringly...

Like pure white heat, my body tenses and begins to convulse as I take all that he is giving me and absorbing the heat of him. His body begins to shudder as he works himself in and out of me when he suddenly stills and explodes within me.

Darkness and warmth surrounds me. When I awaken from my state of arousal, I'm lying next to the love of my life, cradled in his arms, clean and fresh again, and ready for a new day.

Seven more kinks to go...

ELLA DOMINGUEZ

THE 12 KINKS OF CHRISTMAS: IMAGINATIVE & THOUGHTFUL

On the fifteenth day of December, my Lover gave to me, five golden showers. Yes, *golden showers,* but not in the typical sense.

For some, a golden shower in the truest form is alluring. However, my Sir's version of a golden shower is much more intriguing than simply being urinated upon. Though he's literal, he loves to keep me guessing and often, things aren't as they may seem. Because he's imaginative like that.

When I arrive home, the only light shining in the room are the flames in the fireplace. The smell of pumpkin pie is lingering in the air, and a slowly cooking ham that I placed into the crockpot before leaving for work is bubbling in the kitchen. *I do love Christmas.*

I follow the rose petal trail to the master suite where he is waiting, fully erect, and clothed in only his birthday suit.

"What have you been doing?" I ask when he smiles devilishly at me.

He strokes himself twice. "Anxiously waiting for the festivities to get underway."

The love I feel for this man is staggering.

I drop my bag to the floor and lunge at him.

"Not yet. Patience…" He quickly rebuffs my advances.

I have no patience. I want him, and I want him now, but I know his word is law and so, I do as I'm told and wait.

Lying beneath him, he slips my dress over my head, revealing my less than firm, round belly. The sensation of emotion wraps itself around me when he rests his chin onto my abdomen and stares up at me.

"Such a beautiful belly. It will look even more enticing when I put a baby in there." He reaches up and squeezes my breasts. "And these titties are filled with milk."

Yes, I truly do love him and all his strange perversions.

With the ease of a man who has practiced his sexual moves for eons, he removes my panties and bra, lingering at each station as he caresses each part of my body. Like Zeus, the God of Lightening, whenever he moves and our bodies touch, electricity crackles just beneath his skin.

He rises from the bed with me in tow, guiding me to the bathroom. My eyes zoom in on the five champagne flutes filled to the brim and harvest spice scented candles that line the bathtub. The only thing missing from the sensuous equation: water.

He guides me to the empty tub and hands me a glass of champagne. One sip and my taste buds tingle. He's spent a pretty penny on this Möet & Chandon; nearly a week's worth of his modest pay. I smile up at him, grateful for his generosity when it wasn't necessary. His love is enough for me.

Releasing my hair from the bun at the back of my head, he drags his fingers across my scalp to loosen it around my shoulders.

"Not a drop wasted, Butterfly."

I warily eye the five glasses of champagne. To drink this amount will leave me unreasonably inebriated and thoroughly incapacitated.

The most genuine laughter slips past his lips. "No worries. You won't be required to consume all of it. Merely lick it off."

He climbs into the tub with me, his back to my chest, snuggled in between my legs. My sex is pressed into his lower back and the heat of his body makes me throb with need. We sit like this for nearly an hour, relaxing and discussing the day's activities while enjoying the fruits of his labor.

One glass each is all we're allowed for this phase of his plan. When we've consumed our portions, he rises to his knees and faces me.

"How about a golden shower?"

A breathy chuckle rumbles in his throat when I wrinkle my nose at him. When I see the smirk on his face, my apprehension turns to sexual excitement. Reaching for a flute, he drips it down my body. Expecting it to be chilled, I tense up, but he has been kind enough to have allowed it to warm to room temperature. Because he's thoughtful like that.

I close my eyes, relax my body and enjoy my golden shower of champagne.

Drops of effervescent liquid into my navel... A raspy tongue lapping it out. A splash of Möet across my breasts... Teeth tweaking my nipples to a point and his mouth sucking it off. More precious golden beverage poured down my chest, settling on my mound and into my folds... Slurping, sucking and drinking. A champagne-soaked finger dipped into my pussy... His tongue delving for it.

Not a single drop wasted.

"Now it's your turn," his voice is deep and filled with need.

TINY TEMPTATIONS

We trade positions, and I shower my Lover with the same kind of attention, leaving no part of his body untouched by the champagne or my mouth. The mixed taste of his arousal and champagne makes for a heady combination, and my pussy aches with the desire to be filled.

I look up into his heavy-lidded eyes as I take his cock into my mouth, trying to convey my need, but he merely smiles at me. He knows. He senses it. As he always does. I am an open book…

When I've finished dousing and sucking the drink from his shaft, he reaches for me and guides me to straddle him. I lower myself onto his rock hard velvet, taking him slow and deep until I feel the roughness of his pubic hair against my bare pussy.

He sits up, pulling me against his chest as I swivel my hips and grind down onto him. The last glass, he brings to my mouth and tips gently against my lips. I drink, he thrusts. He drinks, I rock my hips. Back and forth, we share the last glass until we reach the peak of our arousal with the scent of sex, champagne and harvest spice all around us.

Our sighs and moans fill the small space and just as we near our release, his lips move over mine, pushing the last sip of bubbly he was holding in reserve, into my mouth.

I swallow, throw my head back and my climax lashes through me. While I'm still shivering from my release, he lifts me to the head of his shaft and pulls me back down. One… Two… Three more times he slams me against his cock and his release crashes against him.

Collapsing into his embrace, he falls backward. Wrapped in his arms, pure energy surrounds me. I'm warm and content. I feel loved. I feel cherished. I feel as if my needs matter to my Lover.

If only Christmas lasted the year long… And it will, so long as we make it last.

Two more kinks to go…

TINY TEMPTATIONS
THE 12 KINKS OF CHRISTMAS: COMICAL & CONSIDERATE

On the twenty-first day of December, my Lover gave to me, an elf costume the color of cranberry.

Whenever he can slip in a bit of his own brand of humor into a kinky situation, he will. Because he's comical like that.

Per his instructions, I've dressed in the two piece outfit while he prepares himself for whatever he has planned next. My stomach is exposed, the short skirt barely covers my pantyless bottom, and my cleavage is overflowing out of the fringed bikini top. If a real elf were to wear this get up, surely they would freeze their nipples and clit off.

When my Sir walks into the room, a laugh bellows out of me. Unintentionally of course, but his grin lets me know that my amusement is welcome. Sexy Santa with a candy-cane dick is the only way I can describe it. The thong he's wearing frames his firm ass, while the upside down candy cane cradles his cock. Atop his head sits a standard-issue, fuzzy red Santa hat.

"Do you ever wonder if Santa fucks his elves?" He beams from ear-to-ear as he stalks toward me.

"Santa isn't real," I playfully back away.

The grin that lifts the corners of his mouth is downright sinful. "Oh, but God is?"

"Yes, that's right."

"Sure, Butterfly, whatever you say," he rolls his eyes.

He lunges toward me and pulls his arm out from behind him, revealing my favorite butt plug. Liberally lubricated, of course; because he's considerate like that.

His eyes shimmer with debauchery when he whirls me around and pushes me down, face first, onto the dining room table.

"Spread those ass cheeks," he demands.

I comply, flipping the tiny cloth of a skirt up and opening myself for him. He presses the medium-size plug against my hole, twists and applies firm pressure. Slowly, smoothly, he works it in. When it comes to rest at the base, the first tiny tremors of arousal begin to tingle in my belly. Just as my loins begin to ache from the foreign sensation inside of me, he spins me back around to face him.

"My name is Santa. Just remember that when you come." He flashes me a sexy, wicked smile that's meant to be both an invitation and a challenge. "Now kneel and suck me off, little worker elf."

On my knees in front of him, my most favorite place in the world, I grip him firmly within my hand, stroking him into complete hardness. A lick... A nibble... His taste is hot and male.

Long, slow vertical movements and the sound of slurping drown out the song *Rockin' Around the Christmas Tree* playing softly in the background. I take him deep until he fills my throat. A growling is heard above me as he thrusts further into my mouth.

His hand on the back of my head guides, leads and directs me. His shaft pulses when pushed deeply into my airway, leaving me gasping for breath as saliva drips down my chin.

He holds my head in place as I drop my hands to my side as an act of complete submission. He owns me. I am his to do with whatever he chooses. He knows this.

Releasing his grip, he allows me to catch my breath only to repeat the process all over. Again and again. Deep... Breathless... Ownership... Submission... Air surging through my lungs and life given to me.

"You're so Goddamn beautiful, Butterfly," he purrs above me.

I open my eyes and cling to this moment, my body sinking into otherworldly bliss. A swivel my hips reminds me of the plug within me and my back arches from the sensation.

"I want to see you fuck yourself."

Though his words are spoken softly, they leave no room for negotiation. Doing as I'm ordered, I slip my fingers into my pussy. There's no need for saliva, I'm already wet. *So wet.*

In and out, his cock, my fingers, the plug shifting inside of me... *So incredible.*

Minutes go by as the searing heat builds within me. I'm pulled to my feet and draped over the table again, face down. He slides himself into my pussy. I'm full. *So full.* His dick buried inside of me, the plug lingering in me... He twists it, tugs at it, pulls it out only to push it back in. His movements are casual and deliberate. He knows how to work my body. One hand on my lower back, the other squeezing an ass cheek, he plunges into me, his grunts of pleasure saturating my senses.

"Goddamn it..." He curses himself. "I don't want to come yet."

"Come for me, Santa," I peek at him over my shoulder.

His eyes light up and his smile crushes me. I've pleased him. That's all I want is to please him; in this moment, in this life and in the next.

He removes the plug and tosses it aside as he dives into my ass at a frenzied pace. He stands me upright, hugging me against his chest as he tears my top away and drops it alongside the plug. Hands squeezing my breasts, teeth on my shoulder, scruff on my neck, a dick in my ass... This is how sex should be – tender and rough all at once, lines blurred and senses overwhelmed.

I won't have it any other way.

"Are you close?" He asks, because he's always concerned about my pleasure like that.

"Not quite," I answer in all honesty.

I press myself against the thickness of his erection, seeking out my release while his hand slides down my belly to my mound and past it. His fingers slick across the small, sensitive piece of flesh at my core, stroking it and tweaking it. It's not long before my release washes over me in a rush of heat and cold mingled with a throbbing sensation.

"Santa!" I moan out as my body jerks and quivers against him.

Rocking his hips, his orgasm follows only a moment later. He fills me with his essence and staggers backward while still inside of me. We collapse onto the couch with his arms wrapped tightly around me.

A jump and a twitch of his cock inside my ass makes us both laugh wildly; because we're silly like that.

I've lost track of how many kinks there are to go...

TINY TEMPTATIONS
THE 12 KINKS OF CHRISTMAS: BENEVOLENT & MINE

My Butterfly is a benevolent creature amongst many other things. She is intelligent, beautiful, and compassionate. Above all else, she belongs to me. Our fate was sealed the moment we first shared a bed. Our first date. Yes, we were eager to be with one another. She opened up to me almost instantly. A lot of women have, but something about her went beyond what the others offered me. Where they gave me sex, she gave me pleasure; where the others sought to satisfy themselves, she sought to gratify me.

She is the submissive to my Dominant. A role we have fallen into. It wasn't easy. No relationship ever is. It took time, but we've grown. Not only as individuals who understand our needs, but as a couple that recognizes and appreciates their partner's wants and desires.

Sadly, our first 12 Kinks of Christmas is coming to an end, but I have no doubt that it's only the first of many to come. I fully intend to make it a holiday tradition that we'll both look forward to every year.

She has far too many fantasies for it not to be a tradition. As do I. Her desires are wicked. As are mine. For that reason, on this twenty-fourth day of December, we'll enjoy two kinks - two that we both share, followed by something *much larger* than anything kinky.

I've left work early to get things in order, and now I'm only left to wait. Right on time, she appears. Her tired eyes let me know that her day at work was stressful, so before we get to the fun; I'll bathe her and massage the tension out of her neck and feet.

Soaking wet and shivering as I dry her, she resembles a fragile animal. Aren't we all just fragile animals, really? Creatures who seek love and consistency? Beings that, when shown kindness, give kindness in return?

She watches me lovingly as I brush her hair, her almond-shaped eyes that are fringed with thick charcoal lashes, seeking my approval and trying to anticipate my next move. But anticipate as she may, she has no idea what's coming. Will she be pleased with my efforts tonight? Undoubtedly.

I've dressed her in something appropriate for the occasion - a dress just short enough to access that coveted possession between her legs, and a sweater to cover her shoulders and keep the frigid night air from making her uncomfortable.

Our conversation is light and playful as we drive to our final destination, the thrill of 12 Kinks bubbling just below the surface. My Butterfly doesn't like large crowds, so our dinner will be at a small out of the way place that offers privacy.

She's beaming tonight. Her eyes, dark as sin, shine against the overhead lamp, the tawny shade radiating whenever she smiles.

I excuse myself to the men's room to text our companion for the evening. Her response is quick and excitement roils in my balls and tingles at the base of my spine. When I arrive back at the table, everything has fallen into place.

"Look who's here," my Butterfly's grin widens at the sight of her close friend and girl-crush.

"What a coincidence," I wink at her enthusiastic girlfriend.

TINY TEMPTATIONS

Her appropriately named friend, *Noel,* giggles and coughs nervously as my Butterfly chats her up. The two of them, both beautiful in their own way, casually touch each other the way women often do. Their eyes roam over one another's bodies and small caresses become friendlier with each passing minute. My Butterfly has taken the bait and my rigid dick strains against my slacks at the mental image of them feasting on one another.

The rush of blood to my cock is unrelenting as Noel sweeps the hair away from my Butterfly's face. They're curious about each other. They have been for some time, but have been afraid to take the next step. I'm happy to help them out. Tis the season for giving, and it would bring me no greater joy than to see the pleasure of my Butterfly fulfilled by someone she has fantasized about.

"Join us outside?" I touch the top of Noel's hand.

As I lead them both toward the back entrance, I grip Noel's shoulders just as she comes to stand underneath the mistletoe.

"Did you know that mistletoe is a symbol of love and friendship in Norse mythology, and that's where the tradition of kissing underneath of it comes from?"

My Butterfly's eyes sparkle with new found knowledge. "I didn't know that."

"Well?" I tug her toward Noel. "We can't break hundreds of years of tradition, can we?"

She gives me a questioning look when, suddenly, the lights go on over her head. She can be so naïve sometimes. And adorably so. The bright red of her cheeks only serves as a reminder of how wickedly sinful her body looks under the exploitation of my flogger.

My mind, perpetually in the gutter… As is hers.

A stutter slips past her lips and her eyes dart between me and Noel. Taking the lead, I direct my response to Noel. "You don't mind, do you?"

"I certainly don't want to be the one to blame for breaking tradition, so by all means, pucker up."

Noel is a good several inches taller than my Butterfly, but it doesn't deter her. She closes her eyes, leans into Noel, rises on her tiptoes and gently presses her mouth to her friend's. The kiss, just a peck really, ends far too quickly and just won't do.

When she laughs and tries to back away, I gently nudge her forward and pin her between Noel and I. "You can do better than that."

"Yes, I think she can," her friend chimes in.

This time, Noel takes the reins and grips the back of Butterfly's neck, tips her head to the side and parts her lips. A soft gasp leaves her mouth when Noel's tongue darts between her lips. Being in such close proximity to the women, I can smell their perfumed bodies and femininity. That in combination with the wet sounds as my Butterfly sucks on her friend's tongue is so Goddamn intoxicating; I lose all blood flow to my brain as it surges to my dick.

The deep kiss lingers for nearly a minute. Being the kind of man who knows a good thing when he sees it, I hate to interrupt. However, if we don't get outside fast, I'll end up with a wet spot on the front of my pants.

I grind my shaft into my Butterfly's lower back. "Shall we take this out back, ladies?"

Her cheeks have brightened to the same shade of red as the berries hanging over our heads, and I can't resist laughing out loud. She doesn't approve and elbows me in the ribs as we all take our festivities to a more secluded location.

The scene is beautiful outside. The restaurant has a small deck under an awning covered in white Christmas lights. The snow on the ground is sparse, and Mother Nature has shown us favor by letting the wind die down. I guess she's eager for the show, too.

The long bench out of view of the other people sitting outside will work perfectly. I take them both by the hand and lead them to it; impatient to get things started.

"What do you want to do first?" I question Noel.

"Can I taste her?" Her eyes glitter against the paraffin oil lamps on the tables.

I glance at my Butterfly. "Would you like that?"

She's nervous and unable to speak, so she simply nods her approval.

Scooting in next to her, I tug her skirt up, revealing her pussy. "Open your legs for her, Butterfly."

I remove my coat, fold it twice, and lay it on the ground between Butterfly's legs for Noel.

"You're such a gentleman," my Butterfly whispers as she reaches over and ghosts a fingertip across my lower lip.

I've been called a lot of things, but never a gentleman. I think I like it.

I wrap an arm around Butterfly's shoulders, while Noel kneels in front of her. A quick look up at us reveals her sinful smile before she finally dips her head down, pressing her face against Butterfly's mound.

"Happy Holidays, Butterfly," I lean into her ear as she begins to pant softly.

"Oh, My Lover. My Sir..." She moans out as her fingers lace through Noel's long locks. "Thank you for this."

"This is for the both of us..." I clarify.

Noel's hands push against Butterfly's thighs, spreading her open while her glistening, pink tongue disappears into my submissive's wet cunt. Feminine high-pitched moans from the both of them make me eager to join in. When Noel sinks her teeth into Butterfly's clit, she bucks her hips upward and lets out the most incredible sound. Sheer fucking delight is the only way to describe it. I reach between her legs and dip my thumb into Noel's mouth and watch her suck it as if it was my cock, then glide it over my Butterfly's clit. Her hand in turn grips me through my slacks as she tries to jack me off through the fabric.

I'm hard so Goddamn hard...

I can't take my eyes off the sexy scene playing out before me. Nor do I want to.

Being the generous person that she is, Butterfly directs Noel to stand in front of her while she slips her hands under her skirt and past her panties. My excitement builds to near boiling point when her mouth captures Noel's clit and she sinks her fingers into her friend's pussy. It only takes a few pumps and licks before Noel's body begins to shudder, and she collapses to her knees.

Pulling Butterfly against my chest, I turn her head to meet my mouth and ravage her, enjoying the taste of pussy on her lips. But the kiss isn't for the selfish pleasure of tasting another woman's cunt, it's to remind her that *I* own her; no one else. And that this is a gift and just because I'm sharing her body, I will *never* share her heart or soul.

TINY TEMPTATIONS

When our lips part, I sneak a hand behind her back and around her waist, hoisting her up into my lap. Another hand pressed under her bottom, and I free my cock from my pants. When she lifts her bottom for my penetration, I push into her.

Noel has readjusted herself but remains with her head dutifully between Butterfly's legs, sucking at her clit while I pump into her.

Two kinks... Fem play and public fucking... This really is for the both of us. Shared fantasies. Shared kinks. Being of like minds, there is a passion inside her equal to my own. We're made for each other in every sense.

Butterfly begins to grind down onto me more rapidly as her orgasm builds. The muscles of her pussy clench and clutch at me, and spasm uncontrollably. She's close and just needs that extra something to push her over the edge. I reach a hand around her body and press her against my chest. Snaking a hand up to her throat, I take complete control of her, enjoying the skitter of her pulse against my fingertips.

"Fly for me, Butterfly," I breathe into her ear as I sink my teeth into her lobe and thrust upward.

The hot, heady scent of her arousal fills my head when her body suddenly jerks against me, and then goes limp.

Noel's tongue circles around my balls and her lips briefly caress my shaft as I pull out, making me grunt. When I do, my Butterfly's eyes light up.

"Your turn," she smiles as she lowers herself to her knees next to Noel.

Together, they concentrate their attention on my painfully erect shaft.

The flick of their tongues in unison… Their lips moving vertically on both sides of my cock… Wet, greedy mouths taking turns at me as if in a friendly competition to see who can take me the deepest... Hands twisting in opposite directions… A tongue swirling around the head of my cock while another laps at my balls… Goddamn…

I take all that they offer and silently demand they give me more when I thrust up into their mouths and push their heads down.

The first tremors of my impending release begin inside my cock, moving along the length of me in tiny convulsive spasms. The rush of heat and surge of blood through my veins overtakes me when the tightness of Butterfly's throat clenches around me, and I erupt.

Quickly, they both lick up every drop of come, leaving me as clean as when I arrived.

My head is still swimming when my Butterfly smiles up at me, reminding me that she loves to please me.

A soft giggle floats up from her throat. "Not a drop wasted, Sir…" But her smile fades as she battles with something internally. "You've given me so much this Christmas. What can I ever give you to repay all of your hard work? What do I give the man who has everything?"

Not everything…

I lower myself to the ground next to her while Noel seats herself on the bench with a knowing expression on her face.

"You've captured my heart, Butterfly. I meant it when I said I planned on putting a baby in that belly of yours…" Languid eyes stare back at me as if she doesn't understand my intentions. "I want you and our children to bear my name." Her eyes widen… It's all becoming clear now… "The only gift I want this Christmas is your promise of forever."

She gulps loudly and tears border her lashes when I reach into my coat pocket. When I pull out a small blue box with a silver bow, she clutches her chest. The ring within it cost me my life savings, but it's well worth it just to see her tears of joy as I place it on her finger.

"Yes, yes…" She stammers as she throws her arms around my neck and nearly knocks me backward. "Forever!"

Noel jumps up and squeals loudly, making a few people glance in our direction.

Helping her to her feet, I hold her close as anticipation thickens the air around us. "Now that we have that settled, shall we begin planning next year's 12 Kinks of Christmas?"

"Christmas?" She huffs. "How about the 12 Kinks of Valentine's Day… And St. Patrick's Day… And President's Day… And…"

Gripping a fistful of her maple-sugar colored hair, I slam my mouth down onto hers, silencing her with my hard kiss, *because she's mine.*

ELLA DOMINGUEZ

HARD CANDY FOR CHRISTMAS

Copyright © Ella Dominguez 2012

TINY TEMPTATIONS
HARD CANDY: LONG STORY SHORT

Lia was in magical limbo. That's what you get when you piss off a witch! How was she to know that the man she threw Pixie dust on was the witch's lover? He had seemed interested and she had been in the mood to play. Now she's stuck in the human realm with no magical powers. She had to break the curse, but she was running out of time! If the curse wasn't broken by mid-night on Christmas Eve, she would be stuck human forever.

Nick and Dale had been friends forever. They had grown up together, had been there through each trial the other had endured. Nothing could separate them. Until they met Lia. The stunning petite woman was everything that either of them had ever wanted.

Would their friendship survive if one of them were to win her heart?

Lia didn't know what to do. She finally met someone that believed she could love. Actually, that wasn't the problem. She had met TWO men that she believed she could love... would one or both of them love her back by Christmas Eve? And if so, what happens when her powers return?

HARD CANDY: ACKNOWLEDGEMENTS

Thanks to Agent99 in my favorite GR group for the story idea and synopsis.

Thanks to all of my Goodreads family for their support and wonderful sense of humor.

TINY TEMPTATIONS
HARD CANDY: CHAPTER ONE

It seemed innocent enough at the time; a little flirting and maybe a little lick and suck if things worked out right. How the hell was Lia supposed to know the gorgeous specimen she threw pixie dust at was the wicked bitch Samara's play thing? If that venomous witch was keeping him happy at home, he wouldn't have been sniffing around her pixie hole in the first place.

Now look what it got her - a cursed existence without her wings and her magic. As if that wasn't bad enough, she had to live with the boring, unimaginative humans, and with their average sized dicks, there was no hope for even a good lay.

Lia lay lazily on her couch feeling sorry for herself and daydreaming of the good old days as she half-heartedly fingered her neglected swollen clit. She had assimilated well amongst the humans considering her circumstances. She was living in a small apartment with an annoying roommate and helping out with her share of the bills.

She was surprised at how quickly she was able to find a job. The fact that she enjoyed it was secondary. As it turned out, answering calls at a 900 number call center and talking dirty helped keep her mind off of her wretched existence.

As she continued to play with her clit, she was mentally kicking herself for being so damned horny. It was the whole reason she was in this mess in the first place.

When she heard the front door unlock, she quickly put herself together and sat up. Her roommate, Phoebe, was home and in her usual boisterous mood.

"So there's a huge costume Christmas party tonight at the Warehouse and you just have to come!"she blurted out a little too happily.

Lia wasn't fond of partying. Human males irritated her. They were always a little too eager to try and get her into bed and often times had their hands all over her. Lia was a natural beauty and with her slim petite figure, large breasts, short auburn hair and beguiling violet eyes, she was a dick magnet. But Lia was bored. It was only three weeks until Christmas and she longed for the touch of a man, and at this point, any man would do.

Christmas Eve midnight for Lia signaled the end of any chance at being turned back into a pixie. Samara's curse would be permanent if Lia didn't find true love by that time. In the beginning, she had searched desperately for a man to love who would love her back, but all of her attempts were ill-fated and after half a dozen failed relationships, she gave up all hope of ever finding a cure for her curse.

Feeling depressed at the thought of being trapped in human form forever, she tried to make up a feeble excuse not to go. "I don't have a costume," she stated weakly.

"No problemo. You can wear one of my old costumes, sweetie," Phoebe told Lia.

Lia rolled her eyes. She wasn't in the mood to disagree or try and object.

Phoebe immediately went into her room and after a few minutes she brought out several costumes for Lia to choose from. She laid them out in front of Lia and then disappeared into her bedroom to get changed.

TINY TEMPTATIONS

Lia sifted through the clothing and was shocked to find a fairy costume with wings to match. It was just a little more than ironic that it would be one of her choices. She quickly took the outfit to her room and changed. Of course, the costume was a bit silly, but it was still suitable. When she put the wings on, her breath hitched and she felt a pang of sadness at the loss of her own. She turned and posed in front of her mirror and then finally sat on her bed, put her face in her hands and began to cry. She really did miss her magical powers and her old life.

After she pulled herself together, she put on some lip gloss and she was ready to leave.

When Lia and Phoebe arrived at the party, it was already in full swing with loud thumping Christmas music, strobe lights and beautiful people in strange costumes dancing and moving seductively to the tunes blaring through the large speakers. There was an enormous Christmas tree in the middle of the dance floor ornate with colorful lights and faux gifts underneath. The smell of pine and cinnamon lingered in the air, along with the mixed scent of different perfumes and colognes.

She made her way to the bar and ordered a caramel apple martini. When she looked up into the mirror on the opposite wall from where she sat, she could see the reflection of a handsome man watching her. She spun her barstool around to get a look at the person who was standing directly behind her.

When she finally came face-to-face with him, she was taken aback at how very appealing he was. He was tall and lean with messy longish dark blonde hair that hung over his eyes and striking masculine features. It was difficult to see the color of his eyes because of the lighting and his hair hanging over them, but they appeared to be dark. He was smiling crookedly at her and kept averting his gaze away from her, looking sideways and not making direct eye contact. Lia also noted that he wasn't in costume like everyone else. Instead, he was wearing a loose fitting pair of worn jeans and a white business shirt underneath a black pinstriped blazer.

As Lia sat looking up at him, he politely apologized. "I'm sorry. I didn't mean to stare at you. You're just so…" he trailed off. He laughed nervously and ran his hand through his hair, pushing it away from his eyes. If Lia wasn't mistaken, he also blushed as he looked around.

"Were you staring?" Lia asked coyly.

Again, he nervously laughed. Lia found his shyness refreshing and very cute. When he shifted his stance, his smell wafted past her nose and she immediately became aroused. He was putting off some serious fuck-me pheromones and her body was responding in a way she hadn't quite expected.

"I'm Lia. Where's your costume?" she asked, trying to make polite conversation.

"I just got off work so I didn't have time to change. I'm meeting my friend here. Oh, and I'm Dale. Are you here with someone?" he asked.

"Yes."

"I see," Dale said as put his hands in his blazer pockets and looked down at the floor.

Lia could sense his disappointment so she clarified. "I'm here with my roommate."

Dale immediately looked up and smiled. "Would you and your roommate care to join my friend and me at our table?"

TINY TEMPTATIONS

Lia liked the idea of joining him, but most definitely not with her roommate. She made up an excuse as she accepted his offer. "I'd love to join you, but I can't seem to find my roommate at the moment. Perhaps she can join us later."

Dale nodded yes and he took her hand as she jumped down from the barstool. The gesture was polite and took Lia completely by surprise. When he touched her, she felt a jolt of electricity and the reaction wasn't just physical; it was chemical. When she looked up into Dale's dark eyes, it was obvious he felt it too by the flushed look on his face. Once again, he nervously smiled.

He led Lia by the hand over to a table at the far end of the room, away from the blaring music. When they approached the table, she was greeted by another attractive male who stood when they arrived. He was just slightly taller than Dale and muscular, with dark, short cropped hair. His eyes, too, were dark, but his lashes were long and sexy, Lia noted. He smiled at her broadly.

"Who's this, Dale?" he asked playfully.

"This is Lia. I just met her and asked her to join us."

"I'm Nick. Nice to meet you," he said reaching his hand out to her.

When she touched his hand, the electricity was felt again. *What's going on?* Lia wondered. Was she just so horny that any male contact was putting her into a frenzy? She immediately pulled her hand away and became irritated with her reaction. *Get control of yourself,* Lia scolded herself.

She sat at the table in between the both of them and they engaged in friendly conversation. It was obvious that they were very close by the way they interacted with each other. It was nice to see two men not afraid to hide their bromance.

"My apologies. We're being rude. Where are you from, Lia?" Nick asked. He was much more assertive than Dale and it was apparent that he didn't have a shy bone in his body.

I'd like to see his assertive bone, indeed, Lia thought lasciviously. She blushed at her own inner dialogue as she tried to answer his question as honestly as she could.

"I'm from somewhere very far from here. I'm sure you've never heard of it."

"Try me. I'm pretty good with geography," Dale chimed in.

Great. That's just what she needed; someone good with geography. She suddenly felt like challenging him so without hesitation she told him the truth.

"I'm from Praeloria."

TINY TEMPTATIONS
HARD CANDY: CHAPTER TWO

Both Dale and Nick furrowed their eyebrows as if they were thinking hard. Nick rubbed his chin like an old professor and Dale cocked his head to the side like a puppy hearing something new. Lia burst into laughter at how adorable they both looked.

"Trust me, you've never heard of it," she told them in between laughs.

"Is it in the U.S.?" Nick asked.

"No," Lia answered.

"Europe?" Dale asked.

"No, not there either," Lia replied. She was quite amused with this little game of 'guess where the pixie's from.'

"Rio De Janeiro?" Nick asked.

"You idiot, Rio De Janeiro is a city not a country!" Dale snorted, throwing his head back and laughing loudly.

Nick looked unamused. "Whatever, Mr. National Geographic."

He looked at Lia and pointed towards Dale.

"This is coming from the man who thought that a blow job entailed pointing a fan at your ball sack."

Lia howled with laughter and Dale immediately stopped laughing and blushed.

"I was 12," he replied defensively, giving Nick the evil eye and a look of shut-the-fuck-up.

"You were not! You were 13!" Nick ratted out Dale.

"So? The point is, I was prepubescent, okay?" he said as he grabbed Nick's beer and took a swig from it.

"Hell, I still don't think you know what a blow job is," Nick said accusingly.

Lia watched in amusement at the banter between the two friends. She was quite entertained. She looked back to Dale and waited for his response. Dale looked as if he wanted to say something snide, but when he saw how attentive Lia was to hear his answer, he decided to leave it alone.

"Hmphh," he said and narrowed his eyes at Nick.

"That's what I thought," Nick said, still trying to get the last word in.

The next hour or so went by quickly as the three talked and laughed. Lia didn't even have to get drunk to enjoy their company. In fact, she only had two drinks up to that point. What she enjoyed the most, was how polite they were to her and how, not once, did they attempt to fondle her or make lewd comments.

"Where do you work, Lia?" Dale asked.

The question caught Lia off guard and she choked and sputtered on her drink. Her eyes scanned the tabletop and she contemplated about lying to him. They were so sincere and the night had gone so well, she didn't want to start the relationship off on the wrong foot. *Relationship?* Lia had to put that thought right out of her head. This was no relationship. It was merely a fun night out with two gorgeous strangers.

"I'll tell you if you both promise not to judge me," she answered as she looked from Dale to Nick.

"No judging here, Beautiful," Nick said and the sweet nickname made Lia's pussy throb.

She swallowed hard and concentrated on not soaking her panties at the look in his eyes.

"I'm a call operator for a 900 number company," she said softly and felt her cheeks heat up. She had never been embarrassed of her line of work before, so why she was suddenly shy was beyond her. Perhaps it was because she really liked these two men and didn't want them to think less of her.

"Like a receptionist?" Nick asked innocently.

"No," Lia said suggestively and raised her eyebrows.

They both looked mildly confused and then simultaneously, the lights came on over their heads.

"Oh, I get it. You talk sexy to men, right?" Nick asked and Lia nodded her head *yes.*

To Lia's surprise, the look in Nick's and Dale's eyes wasn't accusatory.

"Very nice," Dale said and took a drink of his beer.

"Nice?" Lia asked, bemused by his statement.

"Yeah. That has to be a sweet ass job. Are they hiring?" Dale asked as he winked and something in his eyes told Lia that this shy boy might just be a freak between the sheets.

After her confession of her line of work, the conversation continued to flow smoothly. They spoke of Christmas traditions in each other's families, favorite holiday foods, and how they loved Christmas more than any other holiday. Lia felt slightly jealous listening to the two speak so fondly of a holiday which she had never celebrated. Christmas was a human ritual and not recognized in her realm. For Lia, Christmas brought sadness as she thought about her curse. She put her melancholy aside and focused only on Nick and Dale and their joy. It was infectious and something she sorely needed in her life.

As the conversation continued, she learned that Nick worked as a legal assistant and Dale was a junior architect.

"How long have you two known each other?" Lia finally asked as the night was winding down.

"Since the 4th grade," Nick replied.

"We were both interested in the same 5th grade girl," Dale said as a smile stole on to his face.

"So how did that work out for you two?" Lia asked.

"We opted for the friendship instead of fighting over the girl," Nick answered while Dale nodded in agreement.

"Bro's before ho's?" Lia asked and they both looked shocked at her language, but then laughed hysterically at her remark.

When the night finally came to a close, she looked for her roommate, but she was nowhere to be found. Lia suspected Phoebe had hooked up with someone and was already well on her way to her own version of holiday cheer between her legs.

She walked towards the door and Dale and Nick followed behind her like a couple of lost puppies.

"Can I give you a ride home?" Dale asked eagerly.

"No, I can give her a ride home. I'm closer," Nick jumped in.

"How do you know you're closer when you don't even know where she lives?" Dale asked sarcastically.

Lia could already see that there was a competition brewing and she didn't want any part of it.

"Don't worry about it. I'll catch a cab."

They both looked appalled and almost in sync stated their objections.

"No…, no, no…" Dale said.

"Nope. Nuh-uh. No," Nick said.

Lia smiled lamely at how damned sexy they both were. She really liked them both equally and if she had to choose right then who to let take her home, she couldn't do it.

"Fine. I'll let you *both* take me home. We can all ride in the same car together. Agreed?" She said, putting an end to the argument.

They both looked at each other and then shrugged their shoulders as if resigned.

"Who has the fastest car?" Lia asked.

Dale chimed up. "Most definitely that would be me," he said proudly.

"Okay, then we'll take Nick's car," she said, throwing Dale for a loop. "I want to prolong this night as long as I can, if you don't mind." She said, clarifying herself.

They both grinned from ear-to-ear and nodded her decision.

"Smart, Beautiful. Very smart." Nick said.

ELLA DOMINGUEZ

Hard Candy: Chapter Three

The drive went much quicker than all three of them had hoped for and Nick and Dale bid their farewells to Lia. She took down both of their numbers and promised to call.

The drive back to the club to pick up Dale's car was a quiet one. The two would normally be very talkative, but right now they were both sensing a nagging rivalry. It was foreign to them. Their friendship had always come first. They truly lived by the credo of bro's before ho's.

Feeling uncomfortable with the silence, Nick started first.

"So, Lia's pretty special. Wouldn't you agree?"

"Yep." Dale stated.

"Do you like her?"

"Yep."

"Uh-huh. I thought so." Nick replied.

"Do you?" Dale asked and turned his head to look at Nick.

"Yep." Nick retorted.

There was awkward silence again as they both tried to figure out what to say next.

"I'm not just interested in sex with her," Nick said accusingly.

"What the fuck is that supposed to mean? Neither am I." Dale snapped defensively.

"Well, I just know your reputation." Nick said with an undertone of sarcasm.

"And what the hell reputation is that?" Dale asked offended at Nick's suggestive tone.

TINY TEMPTATIONS

"Don't make me say it, Dale. You know - the one where you play all shy and sweet, and then fuck them seven ways to Sunday and dump 'em."

"I never do that intentionally and you know that. I can't help it if we're not compatible. And my shy sweetness isn't pretend. I am shy and sweet. So fuck off."

Nick laughed a little too heartily for Dale's taste and he shot him a look of death.

"Look who's talking. You play Mr. Personality with your go get em' attitude and then you bore them in the sack so much they end up dumping your ass." As soon as Dale said the words, he regretted them when he saw the hurt look on his best friend's face. "Ah, fuck. Nick, I'm sorry. That was a shitty thing to say," he apologized.

Nick shrugged and smiled a little. "It's okay. It's true most of the time."

They both sighed loudly and sat quietly the remainder of the drive. When Nick parked at the club, Dale lingered for a moment.

"So what are we going to do? Just forget about her?" Dale asked.

"Is that what you want to do?"

"Not really."

"Yep, me neither." Nick said.

"Okay. This may sound absurd, but just hear me out. How about we let her pick who she wants to be with? We'll both go on dates with her and let her decide." Dale suggested.

"You're right. That does sound absurd." Nick said, rolling his eyes.

"Why?"

"I don't know. It just seems wrong to be dating the same girl. What if we both have sex with her? That's would be… weird." Nick answered shaking his head. "Unless we make a vow right here and now to not have sex with her until she decides which one of us she likes the best."

"No sex?" Dale looked skeptical at the idea. "How about other stuff? Can we do other stuff with her?"

"Jesus, Dale. Fine. We can do other stuff with her. I just don't want to hear about it, okay? I mean, if I'm going be fooling around with her and so are you, I don't want to hear about it, okay?"

"But we always tell each other everything. Why should it be any different now?" Dale asked.

"Because I don't want there to be some kind of weird contest between us. Speaking of which, whoever she decides to be with, we have to abide by her decision. Right? I don't want this getting in the way of our friendship. Right?" Nick said forcefully.

"Right, right. That would never happen. Right?" Dale asked dubiously.

"Yeah, right." Nick said, though he had doubts himself.

Dale stepped out of the car and wished his best friend a good night and they both shook on their decision.

"May the best man win her heart." Nick said as they clasped hands.

"Yes. And if it's you and not me, I'll be happy for you, bro." Dale said in complete sincerity, though he knew he would be a little more than heartbroken if it wasn't him.

TINY TEMPTATIONS
HARD CANDY: CHAPTER FOUR

Sitting in her room listening to the wall banging sounds of her roommate being fucked senseless by some stranger dressed as Santa made Lia wish she had gone home with one of the attractive men she had met that night. She just couldn't decide which one, even now. They were both smart and funny, and completely appealing in every possible way. She looked at their numbers and wondered which one she would call first. She laid the numbers out on the bed and whispered.

Eenie meenie miney mo
Which eye candy should I call?
Nick or Dale
Dale or Nick
Which hardy candy do I want to lick?

She ended up on Dale's number. So be it. She would call Dale first. She changed into a night shirt, climbed into bed, and dialed his number.

"Yep?" He answered.

"Hi, Dale. This is Lia."

There was a pause on the other end and for a moment, Lia thought she had been disconnected.

"Hi, sexy." He answered.

His voice sounded different on the phone. It was deep and commanding, with a hint of playfulness.

"I just wanted to tell you that I had a wonderful time tonight and that I enjoyed both you and Nick's company. Can I see you again?" Lia wasn't shy about stating what she wanted, though she did hold back the fact that she wanted to ride him hard.

"Absolutely. I'd love that. What about Nick?"

"What about him? I'd like to see him, too," she said, being completely honest.

"I see."

Lia hesitated and wondered if she had gone too far in her honesty.

"Is that going to be a problem?" She asked.

"Absolutely not. We're all grownups. I believe strongly that in order for a person to make an informed decision, they should first explore all the possibilities."

Wow. Lia was impressed. He actually sounded like he meant that, too.

"Thank you, Dale. What possibilities would you like to explore with me?"

Again, there was silence on the other end.

"How about we just get to know each other a little better?"

"Oh, sweet Dale. I should tell you that I'm a very good judge of character and I know that's not what you're interested in right now. You come off very shy and sweet, but I sense there's a very naughty boy behind that façade. I'll be completely honest with you, right now, what I want is to hear your sexy voice telling me exactly what you want to do to me."

Lia swore she heard Dale smile.

Although Lia had lost her wings and her magic, she had retained her ability to see people's life force. She wasn't sure if that a fluke or just something Samara had overlooked, and she wasn't complaining. She couldn't see everyone's life force, only people with whom she felt a genuine connection. As the night had gone on, Dale and Nicks's colors had revealed themselves to Lia, and had shown brighter and brighter.

TINY TEMPTATIONS

Nick's force was the color of the Caribbean ocean - a stunning teal with a core of deep sapphire blue. This she knew to mean loyalty to a fault and a romantic at heart.

Dale on the other hand, had put off the colors of a solar flare with deep oranges and sparks of red. She knew that to mean that he was sensual and passionate.

This was the reason for her indecisiveness. How could she choose one over the other? They were like two sides to a coin. She would just have to decide later which one she preferred. For now, she wanted to explore the *possibilities* of Dale.

"I'm waiting," she prodded Dale.

"To start with, I've been itching to see what color your nipples are. What color are they, Lia?"

Lia smiled. "Pink."

"I thought so. I love pink nipples. I'd love them even better if they were in my mouth. Would you like to have them in my mouth?"

Lia slipped her hand under her night shirt and into her panties. "Mmm hmm," she answered as her fingers found their way into her wet well. She probed and massaged as Dale continued.

"I want to run my tongue along that perfect little body of yours, Lia. I want to taste every inch of you."

This was a nice change for Lia. She was usually the one doing all the sexy talk and she was quite enjoying herself.

"What else?" She moaned.

"You know, we really should be talking about ourselves and not dirty talking, Little Ms. Lia," he answered.

What a tease, Lia thought. "Fine. What do you want to know about me?" She asked as she continued to finger herself.

"Everything, of course."

Lia felt like playing with Dale a little bit. "Okay. I'm a pixie from Praeloria. It's not a country or even another planet. It's a realm all of its own. We co-exist side-by-side with the human realm, but we're not visible to humans unless they truly believe."

"Uh-huh." Dale answered.

"I lost my magic and my wings when I flirted with a witch's lover. That's how I ended up here. Now tell me about yourself," she answered, wishing she could see the look on Dale's face.

"Well, now that we have *that* out of the way," Dale answered Lia with sarcasm oozing from every word. "So you're into role playing, are you?"

Lia laughed out loud and lost her concentration and the slowly building orgasm dissipated.

"Sure, Dale. *Role playing.*"

"Okay, so you're the pixie and I'm the... what?"

"You're the delicious hard candy that I want to lick and gobble up."

"Hard candy it is. Though, I'm not sure what hard candy is supposed to act like."

"You're doing just fine," Lia answered with a giggle.

TINY TEMPTATIONS

HARD CANDY: CHAPTER FIVE

The conversation had gone even better than Lia had imagined it would and it ended with a lovely invitation out to dinner in two nights' time.

When she hung up, she felt a pang of guilt for not having called Nick, as well. It was very late and she promised herself that she would call him first thing in the morning.

She slept well that night, with dreams of wings, beautifully colored auras and pixie dust floating everywhere. She was surrounded by Nick and Dale, as they made sweet love to her. She wanted more. She forced herself to go back to sleep after waking momentarily. It wasn't sweet love making that she wanted from these two, it was hard fucking and debauchery. She wanted to be filled by the both of them at the same time. It had been a long time since she had been fucked hard and by a decent sized dick. As she dreamt of Nick and Dale's mouths on her body, she wondered if they were well hung. She hoped they were. If she had any pixie dust left, she would make sure to bestow them with large packages in order to pleasure her properly.

When she woke, her panties were thoroughly soaked and she felt invigorated.

She lay in bed for a few minutes, thinking about her life as a pixie. She missed it desperately and there wasn't a minute that went by when she was wasn't thinking about her old life: The small cottage she lived in; her friends and family; and the Pixie Guardians who had warned her on more than one occasion to stop her shameless flirting or it would end up getting her into trouble. She knew that her flirting and her previous warnings were the very reason that they hadn't come to her rescue when Samara cursed her. Lia supposed this was the Pixie Guardian's way of teaching her a lesson, though it felt like an awfully harsh way to teach someone the error of their ways, in her opinion.

It was very early and the sun was barely making its appearance on the eastern horizon, but Lia couldn't wait any longer to hear Nick's voice. She hoped their conversation would go as well as it had with Dale.

She dialed his number and waited eagerly. He picked after several rings and the sound of his sexy sleepy voice set her nerves on edge.

"Yes?" Nick whispered in a husky voice.

"I'm sorry for waking you so early, Handsome. This is Lia."

He cleared his throat and rustled around a bit before answering.

"Did you just call me handsome?" He asked mischievously.

"Yes, I did. Is that okay?"

"Gee, let me think about that. YES."

Lia giggled into the phone.

"Shit, Lia. You have an amazing voice. And that giggle? Jesus Christ. I can understand now why you've chosen the profession that you have. You must do exceptionally well at your job."

Profession? Lia didn't consider talking dirty to men a profession. What she did consider it was a fun paid pastime.

"I wouldn't really call what I do a profession, Nick."

There was a pause and Nick's breath hitched.

"I love it when you say my name, Beautiful."

To Lia's delight, the conversation was getting off to a fantastic start.

"And I love it when you call me beautiful. It makes me feel special."

"I don't know you very well, but I can say with certainty that you're special. In more ways than I know, I'm sure."

He knew all the right things to say. Nick's life force was spot on; he was a romantic, indeed. She felt her need to confess to him, though she was unsure why.

"Nick, I should tell you that I spoke with Dale last night on the phone."

There was a pause. She hoped she hadn't hurt him by telling him that.

"I also have to tell you that the only reason I called him first was because he won the eenie meenie hard candy test."

Nick chuckled. "The what?"

"You know, the eenie meenie miney mo thing that you humans do. I improvised it a bit and added the hard candy part."

"Us *humans*?" Nick asked bewildered and amused.

Oops. Lia hadn't meant for that part to slip out. She didn't quite know how to answer him and stuttered a bit. Luckily, Nick chimed in before she was forced to lie or make up some lame excuse.

"And what exactly is hard candy?"

"It's what you and Dale are. You're both eye candy with hard bodies. Hence, hard candy."

"Very nice. I like that. Do you like hard candy?"

Lia was caught off guard with Nick's suggestive question. He was a naughty boy, too.

"Oh, yes. I *love* hard candy." Lia teased.

"Do tell, Beautiful."

"Well, to be very specific, I like to lick and suck hard candy."

"Lia, Lia, Lia. You're a mischievous little pixie aren't you?"

Lia froze. "Why did you call me that?" She had to know.

"Isn't that what you were dressed up as last night?"

Ah, yes. Now it all made sense. Lia felt a sense of relief. Or was it relief that she was feeling? She almost wished he had seen through to her real self.

"So tell me a little about yourself." Nick said, sounding much like Dale.

What was with these two? She thought perhaps they had only wanted to have some fun, but so far, they seemed very interested in getting to know her. She didn't know if that was a good thing or a bad thing. She'd give Nick a go at the truth like she had with Dale, and see what Nick's response was.

"Well, in fact, I really am a pixie. And a naughty one at that. I lost my magic and wings because of it."

"Really? Wait, from Praeloria, right?" Nick said kiddingly.

"You asked, so I told you."

"I see. Well, I've never been with a *real pixie* before, so this should be very interesting. What would you like me to pretend to be?"

Oh, brother. Nick thought she was role-playing, too.

TINY TEMPTATIONS

"You don't have to pretend to be anything, handsome. You can just be yourself and that'll make me a very happy pixie."

ELLA DOMINGUEZ

HARD CANDY: CHAPTER SIX

The conversation with Nick had gone just as well as it had with Dale. She had another date planned, this time with Nick. She was excited to see him tonight. He sounded very eager as well.

Her day at work had gone quickly. With each sexy phone call, she had imagined she was talking to either Nick or Dale, and her enthusiasm showed. When she was called into management's office, they gave her mad kudos for her vivid imagination.

As she rode the bus back to her apartment, she drifted in and out of sleep and wakefulness. Her thoughts were once again on hard candy. She wanted them badly. More than she had wanted any human man. She was mildly confused by her intense feelings for them. She had, after all, just met them. She wrote it off as lack of good sex and hormones.

Her happiness was overshadowed when she saw her human world vaporize around, the edges fraying away and dissolving. The lighting around her became brighter with vibrant colors and when she smelled jasmine and cherry blossom, she knew immediately what was happening. She was being transported back to Praeloria.

She quickly scanned her surroundings wondering why she had been brought home. She only had to wonder for a brief moment when Samara appeared before her.

"You look healthy." Samara said sarcastically as she eyed Lia.

"What the hell, Samara. Why am I here?"

TINY TEMPTATIONS

"I just wanted to remind you of what you're missing out on. Just imagine, you only have a few short weeks and you'll never see this place again."

Lia felt her feet leave the ground and fluttering behind her. She reached her hand back and felt her wings. Tears filled her eyes and she drifted about, testing out her ability to fly, making sure she hadn't lost her touch. Then abruptly she fell to the ground. Her wings were gone once again.

Samara laughed cruelly and Lia stood and slapped Samara hard. She knew she would regret it, but at this point, what else could Samara take away from her?

The slap stunned Samara and she growled obscenities at Lia. When Samara raised her hand and mumbled something under her breath, Lia braced herself for the next round of witchcraft. Lia closed her eyes and envisioned Nick and Dale in all their glorious manliness, and to her complete and utter shock, nothing happened. When she opened her eyes, Samara looked just as befuddled as Lia felt.

Samara raised her hand again and mumbled the same foreign words and again... nothing. Lia was feeling emboldened by whatever was going on and she lunged at Samara and slapped her hard again, knocking her to the ground.

"Send me back, you cruel bitch. I've already been cursed to a life without my magic and wings. I have three more weeks until I'll be rendered human forever, so just get this over with." She yelled at Samara as she stood over her.

The anger coursing through Samara's veins could be felt everywhere as the sky darkened and shadowy clouds swirled around them. The smell of jasmine and cherry blossom disappeared and the smell of rotting flesh filled Lia's nostrils. She closed her eyes and felt a sudden jolt of electricity. When she opened her eyes, she was sitting on the back of the bus again. She felt weakened and out of breath from her encounter with the evil witch. She laid her head back and envisioned Dale and Nick once again and slowly, her energy came back.

The remainder of her bus ride was quick. She made her way down her street to her apartment, anxious about the evening planned out with Nick. When she got to her apartment building, Nick was waiting on the stoop, sitting on the top step. He was smiling and holding a charming bundle of jasmine and cherry blossom flowers.

She was staggered. *How did he know?* She lunged herself at him and cried into his chest. She was still feeling emotional about her encounter with Samara and the gesture from Nick overwhelmed her. Nick hugged her tightly and whispered sweet things in her ear.

"Lia, Beautiful. What's wrong?"

Lia felt embarrassed and sat up, wiping her tears away. "I'm so sorry. This is really embarrassing. I just had a really bad day. I'm not usually like this. I never cry. Really. *Never.*"

Nick looked sincerely concerned and wiped her tears away.

"It's okay to cry, you know. It's good for you. It's a proven fact. A good cry is soul cleansing. I read it on Wikipedia."

Lia's mood promptly lightened at Nick's response. She grabbed the flowers from his hand and inhaled deeply. She was immediately transported back to her childhood home with visions of her pixie friends and old life.

"I'm not sure why I chose these particular flowers. I was driving along and suddenly I saw jasmine and cherry blossoms. It was actually pretty weird."

Lia was shocked.

"When did that happen?"

"Just a short while ago."

Could it have been the same time she had closed her eyes and envisioned Nick and Dale? The moment just before Samara was about to deliver her wrath? Lia quickly put it out of her head. Surely she was overreacting. *It was just flowers, after all.*

The snow was just starting to fall and she invited Nick in, but he wanted to leave straight away. She was hoping to change first, but Nick assured her that she was gorgeous just the way she was.

Their evening was filled with dinner, laughter, and flirting. They drove to the park to see the Christmas lights and listen to the carolers. Finding an isolated park bench, they snuggled up together. The shimmering snowflakes drifted around their heads and melted in their hair, and for the first time, Lia felt the holiday spirit. The light breeze was cool and true to Nick's romantic nature, he pulled Lia close and buried his face in her neck to keep her warm. When he looked up at her, she gave him her best kiss-me-now eyes and was overjoyed when he responded. He put his hands into her hair and kissed her softly. He slipped his tongue inside her mouth and he tasted divine. Lia grabbed his face and kissed him deeper, pushing her tongue inside his mouth and running it along the ridges of the roof of his mouth, their tongues doing a sexy dance as they twisted together.

"You're so beautiful, Lia," he whispered into her mouth.

He slipped his hand underneath her shirt and fondled her breasts seductively and then moved his mouth towards her neck and nibbled and sucked at her. She wanted more. She knew it was too soon to have sex... *or was it*? Whose rules were those anyway?

"I want you..." She breathed to him.

"I want you, too," he said back as he unbuttoned her pants and slipped his hand inside.

His fingers found their way quickly and he slipped them inside of her. She was aroused and damp from their making out and the wet sounds coming from her body were sexy and dirty. He pushed his long fingers in and out of her, burying them deeper inside of her. His thumb found her swollen nub and Lia tried to moan out, but Nick's mouth covered hers and captured the sound before it could leave her body.

"You taste so good, Beautiful," he said in the sexiest voice Lia had ever heard.

She was close. She ground her body into his hand as he continued to tease her clit and within a few short moments, she got her release. She screamed out, the sound of her voice filling the cool night air.

"You look so God damned spectacular when you cum. Has anyone ever told you that?" Nick asked with gleaming eyes and a sweet smile on his mouth.

"No, you're the first."

"I'm sure it's not because they haven't thought it," he replied and Lia felt like a naughty pixie.

HARD CANDY: CHAPTER SEVEN

Once she arrived back at her apartment, she tried to invite Nick in but he resisted, making up an excuse. Lia could tell he was holding something back, though she couldn't put her finger on what.

"What's wrong?" She asked.

"I just think we should wait. I'll call you tomorrow. Goodnight." He answered and kissed her unceremoniously and departed.

Lia was utterly confused. She thought the night had gone so well. Why did Nick rebuff her invite when it was obvious that she wanted to fuck him? *What man wants to wait?*

She put his rejection aside, showered, got into bed and called Dale. He picked up immediately and sounded as if he were out of breath.

"What are you doing over there? Running a marathon?"

"I was working out."

Lia liked the image of Dale toning his lean physique.

"How was your date?" He asked Lia, taking her by surprise.

"You knew about that?"

"Of course. Nick's my best friend and he's very predictable. I knew he wouldn't wait to see you. I also knew he wouldn't allow me to be the first to take you out. He's very competitive that way." Dale laughed.

Lia liked the sound of Dale laughing. She could also hear his loyalty for his friend in his voice. When he spoke of Nick, there wasn't a hint of animosity and it touched Lia.

"I had a nice time with him."

ELLA DOMINGUEZ

"Good. I'm glad to hear that. He's a good man."

Lia was bewildered. These two weren't going to make it easy for her to choose.

"Yes, he is. And I suspect you are, too."

"Well, I tend to agree with you, but I hate to toot my own horn. So tell me something…"

Lia braced herself for the worse. Dale would surely question her about her goings on with Nick and she wasn't sure if she was prepared to tell Dale how Nick had made her cum like a freight train.

"…what are you wearing?" He asked.

"That's what you want to know?" She snorted.

"Yes. Men are very visual creatures. Don't you know that? I don't just want to know… I *must* know. I *need* to know. My life force *demands* it."

Life force? The coincidence was just too much. Lia sensed there was definitely something strange going on with these two. Maybe they had been sent by Samara to trick her. She chastised herself for even thinking such a horrible thing. She would've seen that in their life force colors if they were being deceptive. There's no mistaking the yellow hue of a liar.

"I do enjoy it when you're so determined, Dale. And because I know that you can't live without knowing what I'm wearing, I'll tell you. I'm not wearing a stitch of clothing." She lied, but she fully intended it to be the truth as she slipped off her night shirt.

"You've gotta be shitting me?" He asked dubiously.

"I shit you not, my naughty boy. I'm lying here as naked as a jay bird."

"You're a little tease, Lia from Praeloria."

TINY TEMPTATIONS

"I'm no such thing. I'm a woman of action." She answered defensively.

"What kind of action?" Dale whispered.

Lia could sense his sexual tension and she wanted desperately to satiate it, along with her own. She was feeling sexually frustrated from Nick's rejection and she hoped Dale would take the bait.

"Come over right now and I'll show you what kind of action."

There was a brief pause and heavy breathing on the other end of the phone.

"I'll be right there," he answered and hung up.

She hoped he was serious. She put on her sexiest bra and panties, slipped on a see through tank top and waited. Within minutes, there was a knock on the door. Dale had arrived so quickly, Lia wondered if he had grown wings and flown.

When she answered, he looked magnificent. His hair was a mess and falling in his eyes and the smell of his work-out sweat teased her senses. His eyes moved up and down her body and a smile played on the corners of his mouth. He licked his lips and his aura burned red hot. Lia could barely contain herself. He no sooner made it inside the door and she threw herself at him. He caught her in his arms, lifted her and she wrapped her short legs around his waist. His mouth was on hers and their tongues danced the tango in each other's mouths. She moaned the way to her room.

Once in the room, he tossed her on the bed brusquely, catching Lia by surprise. She started to rise on her knees to undress him, but he stepped back.

"No, no, Lia. You do as I say, and *only* as I say. Do you understand?"

She sat back on her haunches and watched him, wondering what he meant. He started to undress slowly, teasing her with his paced movements. When he got down to his briefs, he stopped and stroked himself through the fabric, growing harder with each movement. Lia was dying to get her hands on him, but he stood just out of reach.

"Lay back and spread your legs." He ordered.

His voice was fierce and powerful, and Lia did what she was told without hesitation. It seemed Dale had a dominant streak and Lia was both surprised and aroused by it. She had never been with a dominant male. She was the one who usually had to initiate things.

He moved between her legs and lifted her shirt over her head. Kissing her deeply, he sucked on her tongue. She closed her eyes tightly and moved her hands up to touch him, but he grabbed them before she could accomplish her goal. With one hand, he pinned them above her head.

"Did I say you could touch me?" He asked with a heated look.

"No."

"No, I didn't. I'll let go of your hands, but I want them to remain at your side until I tell you otherwise. Do you understand?"

"Yes, Sir." She answered, not really knowing why she chose to call him that. Perhaps she sensed that what he wanted. It was hard to decipher her thoughts at the moment because they were so clouded with lust, but she could swear that his wants were being whispered in her subconscious.

Dale smiled mischievously and Lia knew without a doubt, that Dale was pleased with the title.

TINY TEMPTATIONS

Dale slipped off Lia's panties and looked into her eyes and winked.

"I'm glad to see the carpet matches the drapes," he said playfully.

Lia rolled her eyes and he laughed. He pulled her breasts out of her bra, resting them on the shelf of the underwire and pinching her nipples firmly. Lia squirmed while he rolled them through his fingers. He pulled them to a point and sucked them hard.

"Pink, indeed," he groaned.

He kissed her belly and dipped his tongue inside her navel, swirling it around and making Lia giggle from the ticklish sensation. Then he moved in between her legs and kissed and licked her fuzzy mound. He slipped his tongue teasingly into her slit, running his tongue over her throbbing bundle of nerves. Opening her labia with his thumbs, he blew warm air up and down the length of her clit to her entrance and Lia about came unraveled. Her hands moved up to his hair as she pushed it away from his eyes. He started to object, but Lia cut him off.

"I want to see what's going on behind those wicked eyes of yours." She said and Dale quieted himself and grinned.

Without warning, he shoved his face into her wet pussy and started licking and sucking at her maniacally. Lia moaned out loudly and her breathing became frantic. She had never been taking orally in such an aggressive way and she loved it. His eyes met hers while he continued to nibble at her labia and clit, but the sound that emanated from him was her complete undoing. It was a deep growl from his throat and the purring warmness vibrated on her in a way that made her feel wanton and filthy. He dipped his tongue inside her dripping hole as he rocked her pelvis upward to get better access. He slid two, then three fingers inside of her and found her swollen ridge without delay. It only took several tugs and Lia screamed out as she came hard and fast against his hand. Dale lapped up her juices greedily and then moved off of her while she continued to bask in post orgasm afterglow. She rolled over and attempted to straddle him, wanting to ride him, but he gently pushed her aside and stood.

"I should get going." He said, standing and grabbing his pants.

Lia was shocked. He had a massive hard-on and had to be sporting some serious blue balls and he was leaving?

"Don't you want me to finish you off?" She asked, sounding needier than she intended.

He grinned sheepishly and looked as if he was contemplating her offer, but he shook his head *no.*

"I can finish this off myself later. But thanks for the offer." He said politely and left.

TINY TEMPTATIONS
HARD CANDY: CHAPTER EIGHT

These two hotties were turning out to be more of a challenge than Lia had anticipated. No man had ever been able to resist her wiles and now, two in one night? She was too tired to think about it anymore. She drifted off to sleep again, with images of Nick and Dale.

She felt something burning in her heart, something growing in the core of her soul, something that was unfamiliar to her. Lust? Definitely. Desire? Undeniably. Compatibility? Positively. But it was something else. What?

Her dreams that night started out good, but soon, they turned dark and Samara's face invaded them. Her lost wings and magic tore at her heart. Would she ever get used to being without them? Would she ever be able to accept her new life as a human?

"Wake from your sleep little teasing whore, your curse will soon be permanent, and you'll be a pixie no more." She heard whispered in her ear.

Lia woke up with tears in her eyes and her heart pounding to find the witch sitting on the edge of her bed. Her wretched smell filled the room, making Lia gag and choke.

"Why are you here?" She half yelled.

"I don't know what you're playing at, but if you think that you can get out of this curse, you're dead wrong."

Confused by Samara having crossed the boundaries of their realm to give her an inexplicable warning, she asked "Would you care to explain that statement?" With narrowed eyes, Lia glared at

Samara, waiting for her response and barely resisting the urge to slap her again.

"Are you saying you don't know?"

Lia crossed her arms and raised her eyebrows. She was frightened of Samara, but she put on her best poker face. "Go back to where you came from. You're not welcome here. I don't need your threats and I don't need this fear." Lia waved her hand at Samara as if to dismiss her and Samara's eyes widened with alarm.

Lia was shocked to see Samara surrounded by light and then suddenly disappear. *What the hell just happened?* The faint odor of jasmine filled her room and Lia started to shake uncontrollably. Had the Pixie Guardians finally shown her favor and allowed her to perform a spell? She pulled herself together and wobbly made her way to the kitchen as she suddenly felt parched and drained of energy. She had barely gotten a few sips of water down when she fainted.

She felt hot hands on her and her body being moved. There were soothing voices whispered in her ears and the most seductive smell filled her nostrils. When she opened her eyes, she was lying on her couch and both Nick and Dale were kneeling next to her with concerned looks on their faces. They were both disheveled and looked as if they had just awoken.

She sat up on the edge of the couch, puzzled by their presence.

"I had a terrible dream about you. Something was horribly wrong. I tried to call, but you didn't answer." Dale said.

Nick nodded in agreement. "Me, too. I woke to the smell of something wretched and all I could see was your face and you looked frightened. We both got here at the same time."

Dale and Nick looked at each other puzzled by what was going on. Lia suspected that Samara had tried to put some kind of curse on the two and stop whatever bond was growing between them. She was touched that they had both shown up.

Phoebe came walking out of her room, looking troubled as well.

"What happened, girl? I found you on the floor in the kitchen and then these two hunks showed up at the door shortly after." She winked.

"I was just feeling a little light-headed." She kept her answer short, not wanting to worry the three. She walked to her bedroom with both Nick and Dale in tow and they tucked her in. She looked from Nick to Dale and Dale to Nick, waiting to see some kind of jealousy between them, but they both just watched her intently. Each of them climbed on to her bed, Dale on her right and Nick to her left. Nick ran his hands through her hair and Dale caressed her arm.

She had never felt so content or wanted before in her entire life. She drifted off to sleep with the smell of delicious hard candy wafting around her.

***

Once Lia had fallen asleep, Dale and Nick got up from her bed to leave. They hadn't spoken to each other since arriving and they felt awkward.

"I wonder what happened." Dale said, breaking the silence as they walked out to their cars.

"I don't know. It was strange that we both showed up here at the same time."

"Yep. So how was your date with her?" Dale asked

Nick look dubiously at Dale. "Why do you ask?"

"Come on. I'm just curious. Don't get all defensive." Dale said.

"It was *really* nice." Nick answered with a hint of mystery in his voice.

"Oh yeah? How so?"

"I thought we agreed not talk about this?" Nick countered.

"No, you agreed. I want details, so give it up." Dale prodded.

"Jesus Christ, Dale. It was nice, okay. I like her. A lot." Nick said, reaching in his pocket for his keys.

"Yep. Me, too. I saw her tonight after your date."

Nick look surprised. "You did?"

"She called me."

Nick looked hurt. "Did you have…?" He couldn't bring himself to say the word *sex* for fear of what Dale might confess to.

"Did you?" Dale cut in.

"No, we agreed not to." Nick huffed.

"Exactly. Neither did I. But not because I didn't want to. I seriously want to fuck that girl, Nick."

Nick looked irritated. "You ass. Is that all you want from her?"

Now it was Dale's turn to look hurt. "You're the only ass here. I didn't say that. I'm just saying it was hard not to fuck her tonight when I so badly wanted to."

"Oh, sorry. I didn't mean to… I knew this was a bad idea. Already we're arguing over her." Nick sighed. He looked down at the ground and kicked some dirt, and Dale chuckled.

"We're not arguing over her; we're arguing about her."

"I suppose. I'll talk to you later. I'll give her a call later tonight and you do the same. Something's seriously wrong. I can't put my finger on it, but the last few days I've been feeling like something's just very wrong. Or very right. Or both."

"I get it, Nick. I feel it, too. I've had the strangest dreams the last few nights that involved Lia with wings and pixie dust."

Nick laughed out loud. "Well, she is after all a *real* pixie."

Dale busted out laughing, too. "She told you that same story? Well no wonder we're both so hard for her. She's hexed us with her pixie dust!"

HARD CANDY: CHAPTER NINE

Lia woke the following morning with new purpose. Somehow, twice, she had put Samara in her place and it made her feel fabulous. After Nick and Dale had left, she had delicious dreams of the two of them doing lewd things to her. On the bus ride to work, she remembered how twice in one night, she had cum like she never had before. She wanted this feeling to last forever. They made her happy. They made her feel wanted and needed. At that moment, she vowed to do the same for the both of them. She wanted to show them just how special they were and that she really cared for them both.

***

Their first week together was incredible.

Dale had proven himself to be quite the dominant male. He had tied her down to her bed while he fingered her ass and licked her clean. Then he proceeded to give her multiple orgasms. She passed out from sheer exhaustion that night and didn't wake until her alarm went off the next morning.

Nick on the other hand, had proven to be quite tender. He serenaded her with soft music and sweet words whispered in her ear while they danced around his living room. Then he fingered her into oblivion and worked her clit over so vigorously, she felt the effects for the next 24 hours as her nub tingled from soreness, making it very difficult to concentrate at work the following day.

Lia had cooked for each them, something that was new to her. Her attempts were feeble, but they each appreciated her effort, even if they ended up eating out after her burnt offerings.

Dale had enrolled them both in a cooking class, hoping they could spend some quality time together. During the first class, Lia had damn near burnt the school kitchen down after losing her concentration while fixating on Dale's ass and they were both refunded their money and asked not to return.

Nick had taken Lia to a wine tasting seminar. She had gotten so drunk at the seminar, she made a fool of herself by announcing to the entire class that, yes, she was really was a cursed pixie, but not to worry, she had taught the evil, smelly witch Samara a lesson. They all found it quite amusing, most especially Nick. True to his life force, he carried her into her apartment, held her hair while she vomited like a sickly troll, and tucked her in.

By the end of the week, her bond with the two was growing stronger and she was finding it near impossible to decide which of the two she liked better. Some days it was Dale because of his sexy dominance; other days it was Nick with his caring and nurturing side.

In either case, she had never cum so much in seven days. Every night spent with them, their mouths were all over her and their fingers inside of her, but not once, did she have sex with either of them. It was becoming a dilemma. She wanted to be fucked hard by both of them, yet they were turning out to be real prudes.

***

Week two was even more wonderful, although frustrating. They had each finally allowed her see and touch their marvelous dicks. She was thrilled that they were both well-endowed, though with a little pixie dust, she could make them even bigger, she reminded herself. Now if they would just allow her put her greedy mouth on them, she would be even happier.

After a little coaxing, they had both finally given in to her pleading and allowed her to suck them off, though in all actuality, they didn't need much coaxing at all.

Even though she had orally pleased the both of them and jerked them off multiple times that week, still, there was no nookie to be had for the horny pixie.

When she finally had enough of the teasing, she stomped, crossed her arms and yelled at Dale for not being allowed to fuck him. Dale laughed hysterically and hugged her tight with an "Awww, poor little girl wants a big dick inside of her." Lia wasn't amused at all.

She tried a different approach with Nick. She whimpered and whined, and pretended to sniff back tears, saying that she was just so horny she would surely die if she wasn't fucked. To her utter exasperation, Nick responded in much the same way, saying, "Poor little pixie wants her hard candy… awww."

That week ended with a door shut in both their faces.

TINY TEMPTATIONS

HARD CANDY: CHAPTER TEN

Their third week dating started wonderfully. For the first time, Lia was excited for Christmas. She had saved her pennies and was looking forward to shopping for her two handsome men. The shopping also helped to take her mind off the inevitable; the end of any chance at being turned back into a pixie.

She was also coming to the realization that she would soon have to decide which hard candy she would be with long-term. Both Nick and Dale had started to prod her about making a decision. They were subtle about it at first, but the last few days, she could sense their impatience with her indecision. She decided that she would wait until after Christmas as to not ruin the holidays for one of them.

She wondered how their friendship was faring in light of dating the same girl. More than anything, she hoped it wasn't affecting their bromance negatively. She couldn't live with the thought that they would end their friendship over her.

The last few days also brought an unknown emotion to Lia and she suspected it was the one thing she wasn't looking for; *love.* She talked herself out of it, fearing that her love would be rejected by one, if not both, Nick and Dale. It was far too soon to be thinking and feeling this way.

On the Monday before Christmas, she took the day off and ventured to the mall. The mayhem was overwhelming. Being shorter than most people, she found it irritating trying to fight her way through the crowds. Finally, she found a small store in the corner of the mall and found two perfect gifts for her hard candy. She picked out some pretty wrapping and two bows to top the gifts with, and had them wrapped at the mall.

On her way home, she called her two men and made plans for dinner with the both of them. She was hoping that they wouldn't object to having dinner all together.

She decided to walk some of the way home and enjoy the Christmas lights and sights. She was daydreaming about Nick and Dale, wishing they were with her, one on each side, each of them holding her hands. As she rounded the corner to her street, she was pulled into the alley. It was Samara and she looked pissed.

"Do you really think those two pretty boys will fall for you?"

Lia was shocked at Samara's presence and question. She stood motionless, not answering.

"I can tell you with certainty that they *will not.* Your time is almost up pixie wannabe. No more wings for you. You'll never be free. Here you'll stay forever more, a human to the end, for being a whore." Samara laughed.

Lia giggled at Samara. "Why must you always speak in rhymes? Do you have any idea how ridiculous you sound? Now leave me be you wretched witch, I've had enough with you, you make my ass twitch. I can speak like you, and sound just as dumb, but my pretty boys will stay and they'll make me cum!" She laughed out loud at her own humor and mocking. She had grown less and less fearful of Samara as the weeks had gone on; partly because she had accepted her sentence, but mostly because she felt safe with Nick and Dale.

TINY TEMPTATIONS

She walked away from Samara, turning her back to her. Suddenly she felt Samara's hands around her throat from behind and she fell to her knees. She started to see spots in her vision as her throat was squeezed tighter. Samara was mumbling spells and incantations in her ear and she tried to block it out. She envisioned Nick and Dale and slowly her vision came back and Samara's voice disappeared.

She was left sitting on her knees as people walked by looking at her as if she were crazy. Samara had made herself visible only to Lia and hence, the strange looks from the strangers. She gathered her packages and made her way home.

When she arrived, Nick and Dale were already waiting for her. Phoebe had let them. When she stepped inside, Phoebe pulled her to another room and looked concerned.

"They've been arguing the whole time they've been here. I don't know what's going on, but I just thought I should warn you."

With that, Phoebe left, not wanting to be in the middle of the brewing negativity. Lia stood in the hallway, listening to their conversation.

"When did she call you?" Nick asked.

"When did she call *you*?" Dale countered.

"This is bullshit. Why are you here? This is my night with Lia." Nick snapped.

"*You're night?* Says who? You saw her last night. If anything, this is *my night*." Dale snorted back.

And so it had begun. She knew it was too good to be true. She had come between the two best friends and she felt horrible. Samara was right, neither of them would fall for her because she had come between their friendship and she knew they would always resent her for that. She kicked herself for not making the decision from the very beginning. Marching into the living room, she cut swiftly them off before they started throwing punches.

"Enough, you two. I can't do this anymore. I won't be responsible for coming between your friendship. I never should've allowed this to happen. You're both just so absolutely wonderful. There's no way I could've ever chosen just one of you. *Never*. I couldn't do it three weeks ago and I can't do it now. I'm so sorry for putting you two in this situation. It was selfish of me." Her voice had dropped to a whisper and she looked at the floor, unable to look them in the eyes.

She handed them their presents, not knowing what else to do. When she looked up at them, they both look hurt and angry.

"You're both just so amazing. I... I..." She wanted to say the word, but she couldn't bring herself to speak it.

"You're each going to make some girl the luckiest person in the world someday." She said as she choked back tears. "Bro's before ho's, remember?" She said as tears streamed down her cheeks.

Nick and Dale's cheeks flushed red with her words and they looked at each other.

"I have to get some air. You two can see yourselves out. I'm so sorry. Goodbye."

TINY TEMPTATIONS

HARD CANDY: CHAPTER ELEVEN

Nick and Dale were stunned. Lia walked out, leaving them standing alone in her apartment.

"This is entirely your fault." Dale yelled at Nick.

Nick shot Dale a look of death.

"My fault? How the hell is it my fault?" Nick asked incredulously.

"I saw her first and you just couldn't leave well enough alone. You just had to have her."

"You were okay with that up until now. Listen to me you…" Nick almost cursed at Dale and then realized that they had never fought like this. He stopped himself and backed away from his friend. "This is exactly what Lia didn't want."

Dale looked contrite and shook his head. "I know. She's right. You're my best friend and I don't want to lose that, Nick. But I don't want to lose Lia, either."

Nick put his hand on Dale's shoulder. "Me either. But I guess she already made the decision for us."

"So be it. Bro's before ho's." Dale said feigning indifference, though his words were unconvincing.

"Bro's before…" Nick choked back the words because to him, Lia was no ho. "Let's get out of here. We're better off without her."

***

Lia cried as she left her apartment. Samara had won. She was right. Maybe she had cursed them, too, though she didn't think that was the case. It was just good old fashioned jealousy and indecision. Christmas would be spent alone, just like it had been a year ago.

She walked aimlessly for hours, avoiding going home. When she finally arrived back home hours later, she showered, climbed into bed and cried herself to sleep.

Her dreams were tortured. She saw Samara's face again taunting her and reminding her that her time was almost up and that true love would never find her. She saw Dale and Nick waving goodbye, but they were smiling and it soothed her. She knew that being out of their lives, they would remain friends and it was the only joy she could glean from the whole situation.

***

For Nick, the week was painful. He had hoped that he could just push the memory of Lia to the back of his mind, but that was wishful thinking. He thought about her constantly and he had a difficult time concentrating at work.

Even his relationship with Dale was suffering. They had barely spoken since their last encounter at Lia's. They had tried to have lunch a few days later, but they both just sat silently staring at their food and picking at it.

For Dale, he tried immediately jumping back into dating, hoping that another woman's touch would make him forget about Lia. It was a big mistake and had horrible consequences. He was unable to get hard for the woman he brought home; something that had never happened to him before. Finally irritated with himself, he apologized to his date and took her home.

He had dialed Lia's number multiple times, only to hang up before she answered. He didn't even know what he would say to her if she had picked up. This was supposed to strengthen he and Nick's relationship, but instead, it had the opposite effect and he couldn't bear the sound of Nick's voice because it reminded him of Lia. The gift she had given him sat unopened as he had been unable to bring himself to face what she had gotten him.

On December 23, finally being tired of brooding, Dale mustered up the courage to go his best friend's house and confront him. He showed up unannounced and found Nick sulking as well. He looked as bad as Dale felt.

"I can't take this anymore. I miss you and I miss Lia. I don't know what we should do." Dale said.

Nick's eyes glossed over and he hugged Dale, taking him completely by surprise.

"I miss you both, too. I've been a mess, bro."

Dale looked over at Nick's dining room table and saw Lia's unopened gift. He reached into his pocket and pulled out his gift.

"Let's open them together." Dale said.

Nick looked sullen and shook his *no*, but Dale walked over, picked up the gift and handed it to Nick. Resigned, Nick agreed.

They each tore into their beautifully wrapped packages. Each of them pulled out a commemorative gold coin and a note.

On Dale's note was written: To my sexy, dominant hard candy. You're one side of the coin that speaks to my heart. You make me happier than I've ever been as a human or as a pixie. I crave your touch beyond anything I can explain. I need you both.

On Nick's note was written: To my romantic, loyal hard candy. You're the other side of the coin that speaks to my soul. Whether I'm human or pixie, I can't imagine my life without you. I want you more than I can explain. I need you both.

They were both left reeling. She wanted and loved them both; it was obvious from her words, even though she didn't state it. They both looked each at other and then felt completely guilty that they had put her in a situation where she was made to choose. They were the selfish ones, not her.

Nick looked at Dale and asked, "Now what?"

HARD CANDY: CHAPTER TWELVE

The rest of the week went by painfully slow for Lia. She went through the motions every day. Wake up, work, go home, cry, sleep; repeat. She missed her hard candy and didn't know if she would ever get over the loss.

She drifted in and out of fits of crying to fits of self castigation. She knew better than to allow herself to become emotionally involved with a human, let alone two. It wasn't her plan to become so attached to them. She had only wanted to have some fun and to get laid, and that didn't even happen. She was disgusted at herself for being so sad when she hadn't even gotten a fuck out of them.

She sat picking at her dinner at a local diner, dreading going back to her lonely apartment. Phoebe had gone home for the holidays and she was left to spend Christmas Eve and Christmas day in self-imposed solitary confinement.

She left, having eaten only a few bites and made her way home. It was December 23rd and she wondered what the rest of her human life would bring. Would she ever find love? Would she ever find someone to love her and who would believe that she had once been a pixie? If Samara were here, Lia swore she would kick her ass sideways for her overly harsh punishment for merely flirting with her lover.

Where were the Pixie Guardians when she needed one, anyway?

As she approached her apartment, she was taken aback at seeing Dale and Nick sitting on her front stoop. Standing at the bottom of the stairs, they both rose and greeted her with weak smiles. She had to pinch herself to make sure she wasn't hallucinating. The snow was starting to fall again and she thought to herself that they both looked angelic with the snow floating around their heads like halos and she briefly wondered if Samara was playing a cruel joke on her.

"Can we come in?" Nick asked politely.

"Of course." She said as she pushed past them and opened the door.

They walked in, shook their shoes off and removed their coats and Lia was immediately hit with their scent. It was a delicious combination of both Nick and Dale, and much more appealing than just each of their scents alone. Her body responded with a flutter deep in her lower belly and a quiver in her pussy. She closed her eyes tightly and concentrated on not coming undone.

Nick and Dale looked at one another, confused by Lia's response.

"Are you okay, Beautiful?" Nick asked, forgetting that they had broken up.

Lia's eyes popped open at his nickname and she looked him up and down warily.

"Why are you two here?" She asked defensively. She was starting to think that perhaps this was one of Samara's cruel tricks.

Nick and Dale stuttered and shuffled around looking like a couple of nervous teenagers on prom night. Dale ran his hands through his hair, pushing it back from his eyes and Nick scratched his head as if thinking of what to say.

Lia crossed her arms, sighed loudly and tapped her foot.

TINY TEMPTATIONS

"Are you of couple of Samara's cronies? Because if you are and I've asked, you have to tell me. So are you?" Lia demanded.

Nick and Dale's eyes rounded with confusion.

"Who's Samara?" Dale asked.

"The witch who cursed me. Like you don't know." Lia was convinced that they were, in fact, trolls in disguise.

"Have you been drinking?" Nick asked.

Lia was horrified at the question. "I'm only going to ask one more time. Were you sent here by Samara? One more lie and you'll both be sent back to Praeloria and transformed back into the disgusting trolls that you are. So answer me, damn it."

Dale laughed under his breath. It was infectious and Nick chuckled with him.

Lia narrowed her eyes at them and pointed towards the door. "Get out trolls! I don't need this kind of shit. For your lies, you'll be sent to the pit! Out, out now! Get out, you hideous trolls. May you be cursed like me and be rendered to have no souls!" She closed her eyes and waved her hand hoping her feeble attempt at a spell would work and the Guardians would once again show her mercy.

When she opened her eyes, Dale and Nick were still standing in front of her with huge grins on their faces. She waved her hand and flicked her wrist again, more animated, but still - nothing.

"Oh, to hell with it. Just get out." She said angrily.

Both Nick and Dale burst into howling laughter.

"We missed you, too, Beautiful." Nick said in between laughs.

Immediately, Lia was struck with a wave of energy and the scent of jasmine and cherry blossom.

Light surrounded Nick and Dale and it was then that she realized, it was really her hard candy in front of her. Their sincere joy in seeing her overwhelmed her and she lunged herself at them and hugged them. She started bawling like a baby and then proceeded to slap each of them.

They were both shaken by her reaction. First it was joy, then punishment.

"What the hell?" Dale asked as he touched his warmed cheek.

"You assholes. I've been miserable without you. Now you're laughing at me? You're assholes." She said pouting and crossing her arms.

Nick snickered again. "Like I said, we've missed you, too."

"Seriously, why are you here?" Lia demanded.

"Because we missed you. How many different ways do we have to say it?" Nick huffed.

"We're miserable without you, too. We want you back." Dale replied.

"*We*?" She asked uncertain of Dale's statement.

"Yes, *we*. *We* want you. *We* need you." Nick said with his eyes glossing over.

"I don't understand. I thought you two had decided to move on?" Lia asked.

"No, you decided that. We weren't really given a choice, now were we?" Dale said defensively.

"I did it to save your friendship." Lia retorted back just as defensively.

"Well, it hasn't done us any favors." Nick replied.

Lia looked hurt. "I never wanted to come between you two. You have to believe that."

"We do believe you. So we've decided that no matter what you decide tonight, we're okay with it. So here we are, asking you, who do you want to be with?" Nick questioned Lia.

Lia was shocked. They were still asking her to choose? How thick were these two?

"I'm not choosing. I won't. *I can't.* I thought I made that abundantly clear. I want you both. If I can't have you both, then I don't want either of you," Lia said, sniffing back tears.

Dale and Nick were astounded by her answer.

"You want us both? *Both*?" Dale asked.

"You can't ask us to share you." Nick replied.

"What do you think you've been doing all this time? You *have* been sharing me, you big dopes." Lia rolled her eyes, stunned by their collective ignorance.

Dale cocked his head to the side and Nick scratched his chin like an old professor and Lia was reminded of the first night she met them.

"I want you both." Lia reiterated in hopes of helping them to see her side. "I need you both." She said more fervently.

Their eyes softened and she could see the wheels turning in their heads.

"Think how wonderful it will be. No secrets. No competition. Just the three of us together in every sense." She was doing her best to make her case.

She saw light around them again and the wonderful smell of home drifted past her nose. They both smiled at her and she knew she had convinced them.

"I want you both right now. I think you've made me wait long enough. Don't you? I'll consider having you both at the same time an early Christmas gift."

She looked down at both of their firmly pressed packages in their pants and could see them growing harder. Dale walked over and caressed her face and kissed her deeply. When she opened her eyes to look at Nick's reaction, his eyes were narrowed, but not out of anger; out of pure lust. He walked over and stood behind Lia and kissed the back of her neck while he squeezed her breasts and Dale continued to kiss her mouth.

Nick pressed himself firmly into her ass and she could feel that he was fully erect. When she reached down to Dale's cock, it, too, was completely hard.

Nick pulled Lia's top off over her head and unbuttoned her bra. Dale bent down and sucked at them, while moving his mouth down her belly and unbuttoning her pants. He slid them down her legs and pulled her panties off. She felt Nick squeeze her ass cheeks. Dale's hot tongue was inside of her before she had a chance to realize what was happening and almost simultaneously, she felt Nick's hot tongue in her ass from behind.

She put her hands in her hair, feeling overwhelmed with arousal and desire. Was she dreaming? This was all too good to be true. They had hardly put up a fight at all. Perhaps because they knew it was inevitable. Nick stood up and whispered in her ear.

"I want to be inside you."

She opened her eyes and looked down at Dale who was watching her keenly. When he heard Nick's whispered words, he smiled and stopped licking.

"Me, too."

Lia kicked her clothes to the side and led them both to the bedroom as they stripped along the way. When they got into the bedroom, they were both gloriously naked with erections pointing skyward.

TINY TEMPTATIONS

"I guess I get two north poles for Christmas." She told them and they both laughed out loud.

Nick approached her first and kissed her mouth deeply, pushing his tongue past her lips and swabbing her tonsils. She could hardly wait until that long delicious tongue of his was inside her ass again.

Dale lay on the bed and guided Lia over to him. He magically produced a condom and Lia wasn't surprised at all. Leave it Dale to always be prepared for sex. Nick looked embarrassed that he didn't have one, too, but Dale opened his other hand and smiled as he gave it to his best friend.

"I always got your back, bro." Dale said to Nick. Nick flushed a deeper shade of red and Dale rolled his eyes and chuckled.

Lia was happy to see the two getting along so well under the current circumstances. Dale guided Lia to sit on top of him and lean forward.

"I'll take the front if you take the back," Dale told Nick.

Nick's eyes gleamed with wicked insinuation.

"I've never done that before." Nick admitted.

"I know. Just a word of advice, use some lube for Lia's sake."

Lia immediately pointed towards her night stand drawer and Nick eagerly got it out. He lubed up his finger while Lia slowly pushed herself onto his slickened digit.

"Christ, you're tight." Nick said breathlessly.

Dale cranked his head around Lia to watch his best friend's joy as he played with Lia's ass. Lia whimpered with each thrust of Nick's finger. Then he inserted another finger and Lia's panting got louder. She moved her hand down to Dale's cock and started to stroke him while Nick prepared her ass. She wanted to wait and have them both enter her at the same time. It only seemed appropriate for them to have her together for the first time, at the same time.

"I'm ready now," Lia told Nick.

He moved behind her as she laid her chest on Dale's chest and slowly lowered herself onto Dale's erection. Dale let out a deep sigh and pulled her down hard by her hips. Just as she felt Dale hit her cervix, she felt the fullness of Nick's dick inside her ass. She gasped out and yelped, but then began thrusting back onto Nick and gyrating her hips into Dale's hardness. The wet sounds filled her bedroom and the smell was intoxicating. All three of their sex mingled in the air like something otherworldly. Lia closed her eyes tightly as the pain and pleasure set every nerve in her body on fire.

Nick pulled her up and against his chest, pushing his cock to the hilt and pinching her breasts. He bit savagely into her neck while Dale dug his fingers in her fleshy curvy hips and pulled her down hard onto himself as he thrust upwards. She cried out their names as she felt near orgasm. Dale's hand moved to her slit and he slid his thumb inside her labia where he fingered her clit vigorously.

Lia's breathing quickened and her whimpers got louder.

"Cum for us, Beautiful. Show us how beautiful you look when we both make you cum." Nick whispered in her ear and it completely unraveled her.

She screamed loudly as she came hard and fast. Her body was still quivering from her orgasm as both Nick and Dale pounded into her. Just when she thought she couldn't take any more, the warm sensation of another orgasm filled her clit. It started slow and then built up and her body shook again with another release.

"Ah, fuck!" Nick growled deeply as he felt Lia's tight canal clamp down on him again. He stilled and then grunted with his finish.

A moment later, Dale pulled himself up to face Lia, got a wild look in his eyes and let out a string of obscenities that shocked both Lia and Nick.

"Motherfuck, fuckity fuck, fucking hell... Jesus H. Christ!!" He yelled and then fell back onto the bed panting wildly like a rabid animal.

Lia rolled off of Dale and burst into loud laughter and Nick grabbed his stomach and hooted with laughter, as well.

HARD CANDY: CHAPTER THIRTEEN

After Lia's fit of laughter, she dozed and drifted off to sleep. Her dreams were wonderful and filled with images of hard cocks, pixie wings and magical spells, and rivers of delicious cum.

"Mmmm..." she heard herself mutter.

When she opened her eyes, Dale and Nick were on either side of her, watching her fixedly.

"I thought maybe it had just been a fantastic dream," she whispered.

"No, Beautiful. This is real life." Nick whispered as he lay next to her, propped up on one elbow.

"Uh-huh. Reality. Though a different kind of reality for all of us, I think." Dale said, and his words rang true.

This was a completely new experience for all of them. Nick and Dale had shared everything about their private lives for as long as they could remember, but this was different. Lia was surprised that they seemed to be doing so well in sharing her. She wondered how long it would last.

"I want this to last forever." As soon as she said the words, she regretted them, fearing their rejection.

"Why can't it?" Dale asked, stunning Lia.

"I don't know. It just seems too good to be true," she said sadly.

"Oh, Lia. Always the skeptic, aren't you. It will last as long as our hearts desire, Beautiful." Nick said dreamily.

Exhausted, they all drifted off to sleep.

TINY TEMPTATIONS

***

The next morning, Lia woke to find her hard candy gone. She felt depressed. Perhaps it was just a dream. Perhaps they had decided that she was only good for one thing. Perhaps they had decided that sharing her would be too much of a strain on their friendship. Perhaps... Lia gave up on the perhaps and got showered. She changed her bed sheets and cleaned up her strewn clothes and sat on the edge of her bed, feeling gloomy again. They could've at least told her goodbye.

She went out into living room and made herself a cup of hot chocolate and gazed out the window at the snow coming down heavily. It must've started sometime in the night as there was already more than a foot of soft powder covering the ground. It was so serene looking. It reminded her of Fall in Praeloria when the leaves would fall off the cherry blossom trees and layer the ground in a wonderful pinks and white. As she sipped the cocoa, the door flung open and Dale and Nick entered, encased in snow and shivering from the cold air.

She put her mug down and engulfed them with hugs and warm wet kisses, then proceeded to slap each of them. They were dazed at her response.

"I thought you two had left me." She yelled.

"Christ, Lia. Why would we do that?" Dale asked, rubbing his flushed cheek.

"You could've left a note or said goodbye you big goons." Lia looked down at their hands and they were both holding small prettily wrapped boxes. She smiled ear-to-ear and clapped her hands and jumped and down like a child.

"For me?" She asked coyly. "Can I open them now?"

"No, no, Beautiful. Not until Christmas morning." Nick teased.

"Boo," she pouted.

The rest of the afternoon and night was spent lazing around half naked, spooning, and snacking on each other. Lia was quite thrilled to be able to give Nick head while having her pussy eaten from behind by Dale. *A girl could get used to this kind of life*, she thought.

They joined her in the shower and she washed them down thoroughly. Then she got a good ass reaming from Nick while she jerked off Dale.

Nick was turning out to be quite good at anal activities and she was pleased at what a quick learner he was. Dale was a good teacher to his less than experienced friend and they both seemed to take joy in this new stage of their friendship.

As bedtime neared, another fuck session ensued, this time with Dale in her ass and Nick in her cunny. She never knew she could be so bendy and flexible, but was quite pleased with herself and pretzel-like abilities. This time, she requested they both come on her face, tits and belly. She got no objection out of them and they complied like good little naughty angels.

While she cleaned up in the bathroom, Nick and Dale prepared their surprise for her.

She came back out to find them sitting on the edge of the bed, half clothed, and with their gifts in hand.

"I thought I had to wait until tomorrow?" She asked.

TINY TEMPTATIONS

"It's close enough." Dale said.

"And we couldn't wait any longer ourselves." Nick chimed in.

Lia did the eenie meenie miney rhyme in her head to decide which to open first and Nick's gift ended up being first. Nick smiled wickedly at Dale, and Dale rolled his eyes.

Nick's gift was wrapped in shiny royal blue paper with a beautiful teal bow. *How appropriate*, she thought. She was staggered to see a white gold charm bracelet with trinkets that ranged from wings, fairies, and castles.

"For my little pixie at heart." He whispered.

Lia's eyes filled with tears as Nick placed it around her petite delicate wrist. She kissed him and thanked him.

Then she opened Dale's gift which was wrapped in a deep red shimmering paper with a tangerine orange bow. Again, *how appropriate*, Lia inwardly smiled.

The second gift was just as heartwarming and stunned her. It was a gorgeous white gold necklace with a heart pendant with wings and single diamond in the center.

"For my little pixie at heart." Dale growled.

Lia's tears streamed down her cheeks as he placed it around her neck. This was really too good to be true. She attacked them both, stripped them down and ravaged them.

"I guess she likes the gifts," Nick smirked as he looked over at Dale.

"I'd say that's a resounding yes." Dale laughed.

Hard Candy: Chapter Fourteen

After fucking like sex deprived war heroes, they fell asleep from sheer exhaustion.

Lia's dreams were again of Praelora. The smell of home filled her nose and she could feel her feet leave the ground. She could feel air rushing past the back of her neck from the fluttering of her wings. She felt the sheets fall to her feet and it was then that she realized, she wasn't dreaming at all. She opened her eyes and saw Dale and Nick below her, sleeping peacefully. She hovered above them, not paying attention to her flight pattern and hit her head on the ceiling above her and fell back down to the bed, landing horizontal to the way Nick and Dale were laying. They grunted with the thud of her body hitting them and they were both startled awake. Dale immediately bolted out of bed and was ready to fight, while Nick pushed Lia behind him to protect her.

They both looked wildly around the room. Dale flipped the light on, scanning the room for an intruder.

"What the hell was that?" He asked, rubbing his eyes.

"Shit, I don't know." Nick answered, scratching his head and then his balls.

"It was me. I fell." Lia said, still trying to comprehend what had just happened. She reached behind her and felt her wings and gasped. It was true. Her wings were back. But how? Then it hit her - she had found true love. She was so taken with their show of affection that she had completely forgotten about the time or her curse.

TINY TEMPTATIONS

Nick turned to face her and looked confused. Dale shook his head as if puzzled by her answer, too.

There was no hiding the truth anymore.

"I'm a pixie again. My curse is broken." She whispered, feeling embarrassed, though she wasn't sure why. She just hoped that they wouldn't laugh at her again.

"Lia, enough with that..." Dale started in.

"It's true, Dale. You both have to believe me. The curse was broken. Samara's curse was broken!" She stated more emphatically as the realization started to sink in.

"Oh, Beautiful, you're still half asleep." Nick said sweetly.

Lia stood and turned her back to them. She turned her head to the side to see the looks on their faces.

"Does this look like I'm still sleeping?" She glared at them.

Their eyes widened and their mouths dropped open in shock.

"What the fuckity fuck?" Dale breathed out.

"Holy Mother of Mary." Nick whispered.

"Jesus H. Christ," Dale said a little louder.

"Fucking Moses, Noah and Joseph." Nick said even louder yet.

"Fuck, fuck... FUCK!" Dale yelled.

"Son of a ...." Nick started to say, but Lia had heard more than enough profanities from them.

She promptly slapped Nick and quickly walked over and slapped Dale.

"Snap out of it boys! I'm a pixie. You've been fucking a pixie. What part of that don't you understand? I've been telling you this all long. Now suck it up and tell me right now if you're okay with this?" Lia huffed at them.

They both rubbed their sore cheeks and remained stoic and stunned.

"I'm waiting," Lia said as her feet started to leave the ground. She drifted around the room, unaware of her actions.

"We've been drugged. That's it. We're high on PCP or something." Nick answered.

"Both of us? How can we both be seeing the same hallucination?" Dale asked.

"Oh, for the love of trolls. I'm a pixie. I. AM. A. PIXIE." Lia said as a wide smile crept onto her face. She felt her cheeks flush and she began to giggle with joy. "My curse is really broken. It's really broken. Fuck Samara!" She said as she began to cry with joy.

"I love you Nick and Dale. And Dale and Nick. And, and… I love you both!" She hooted loudly, not caring what they thought anymore.

They both began to smile, realizing that they were in fact, in love with a real life pixie.

"What was the curse exactly," Dale asked as he sat on the edge of the bed, watching Lia float around the room.

"That if I didn't find true love by Christmas Eve, I would be cursed to be a human forever."

"Cursed? Why is being a human so bad?" Nick asked, hurt.

"It's not. It's just not as marvelous as being a pixie." She said, smiling kindly at him.

"I see," Nick replied.

"So does this mean you're leaving us to go back to Praeloria?" Dale asked troubled.

TINY TEMPTATIONS

With his question, both Dale and Nick looked panicked. It struck Lia that she would have to choose now, to stay in the human realm or go back. How could she leave the two loves of her life? She couldn't. She would just have to be a pixie in the human realm. It would be difficult, but it would be an exciting new challenge that she knew she could overcome with the help of her Hard Candy. She could hardly wait until she saw Samara again to dole out of some of her own punishment on her. This time, she knew the Pixie Guardians would be on her side. But that was neither here nor there. For now, she welcomed her new life and the thrilling new possibilities it would bring.

"Oh, my beautiful Hard Candy, you've given me the best Christmas gift ever; you've given me my wings and magic. How can I ever repay you? I can give you anything you want now. Just tell me and I'll give it to you." She said sitting in between them and pulling them close together in a big family hug.

"I wouldn't mind having a bigger dick." Nick said.

"Hell yes. A bigger dick for me, too." Dale said.

Lia hooted with joy and jumped up and down on the bed between them. So it was big dicks that her Hard Candy wanted for Christmas.

"What a wonderful idea. Why didn't I think of that?" Lia said coyly as she laughed wickedly.

ELLA DOMINGUEZ

MORE FROM ELLA D.

Submission (The Art of D/s Rewritten, Book One)
Domination (The Art of D/s Rewritten, Book Two)
Control (The Art of D/s Rewritten, Book Three)
Becoming Sir (An Art of D/s Novel)

Continental Breakfast (Continental Affair #1)
Continental Beginnings (Continental Affair #2)
Continental Life (Continental Affair #3)

Grace Street (Chapter 8, #1) – Dark romance
Return to Grace Street (Chapter 8, #2) – Dark romance

Altered State – A stand-alone, psychological thriller

Ulterior Designs (House of Evans, Book One)
Interior Motives (House of Evans, Book Two

Hard Candy for Christmas
The 12 Kinks of Christmas
A Cub for Christmas
Adam's Apple
Tennessee Moonshine

Bodega Nights (Toro Canyon, Book #1)
Wine on the Dance Floor (Toro Canyon, Book #2)
Uncorked (Toro Canyon, Book #3)
Kincaid Legacy (Toro Canyon, Book #4)

TINY TEMPTATIONS

ABOUT ELLA D.

In addition to being a writer, Ella is a mom, a wife, a respiratory therapist, and a lover of ukuleles and unicorns. She was born and raised in a sexually conservative, strict Christian household in the Bible Belt of the USA. This upbringing and repression contributed to her wicked imagination, and writing has become a pleasurable and satisfying outlet for her fantasies. At the mature age of forty, she mustered up the courage to share her thoughts and put pen to paper. She sincerely hopes to find her niche in writing romance in all forms, be it dark romance, romantic comedy, psychological thrillers and paranormal.

She doesn't consider herself an author, rather, an avid reader above all else and someone who simply writes the stories that the characters in her head tell her to.

Blog: www.elladominguez.blogspot.com
Twitter: https://twitter.com/ella_dominguez
Tumblr: http://literarysmutologist.tumblr.com/
Facebook: www.facebook.com/theartofsubmission
Goodreads: www.Goodreads.com
Website: www.bondagebunnypub.com
Instagram:
https://www.instagram.com/ella_dominguez/

To listen to the playlists for these novells & more, follow Ella D. on Spotify:
https://open.spotify.com/user/12146676013

Sign up for updates and exclusive teasers:
Newsletter: http://eepurl.com/bwsvUf

Made in the USA
Columbia, SC
15 October 2024